OCT 2009

Praise for *A Soldier's Ride*

"As a career military member and one who served in Vietnam, I found myself absorbed in *The Soldier's Ride* from the first words. The impact we can have on the lives of others, frequently without realizing it, is a subject I've long been interested in and spoken about. Edie Hand with Jeffery Addison's words give us an inspiring example of this, the strength we may unexpectedly draw from others in our greatest hours of need, and of true heroism. It's a book to read, remember and reflect about and I've done all three.... I hope your book sells even a 10th as well as *The Shack*."

—**Wilma L. Vaught**, Brig General, USAF Ret.,
President of Women's Memorial Foundation,
Washington DC.

"A series with important messages for these times about the value of affirming love and renewing faith in families."

—**Dr. Judy Kuriansky**, Ph.D. psychologist, TV and radio commentator and top-selling author of *The Complete Idiots Guide to A Healthy Relationship*

"Edie Hand, and her co-author Jeffery Addison, have done it again. Their new book, *The Soldier's Ride*, is a moving tale of Christopher Lawrence, a young soldier who, after returning home from World War II with severe eye injuries that left him blind, prolongs his emotional healing by pushing away those who love him most. One of those he pushes away is Marie Benedict who has never stopped loving him, challenges or not. Edie Hand knows how to write about challenges because she has overcome many of life's challenges herself. One can't help but hear her own heart and strength come through the pages of this book."

—**Martha Bolton**, former writer for Bob Hope and the author of over fifty books, including *Didn't My Skin Used to Fit?*

"The Ride series are refreshing stories which take us back in times of our lives that we tend to forget in the hustle and bustle of today's world. I highly recommend the series. They are beautiful journeys".

—Tonya S. Holly,
Writer/Director/Producer Cypress Moon Studios

"*The Soldier's Ride* is an inspiring story of faith and love. I love the portrayal of the angels who visit Diana Meade and change her life. The book presents the tremendous rewards of perseverance and prayer. You will want to identify with Marie."

—Lila Hopkins, award-winning author of inspirational fiction, including *The Master Craftsman*

"Edie and Jeffery show us in this series that our journey is made up of many short, yet memorable rides. These novellas offer us simple, powerful lessons to fuel us on those future rides."

—Joey Kennedy, Pulitzer Prize-winning editorial writer for *The Birmingham News*

The Soldier's Ride

A NOVELLA

Inspiration from Desperation

Other Books with Edie Hand

A Christmas Ride: The Miracle of Lights
The Last Christmas Ride
Genuine Elvis
The Unexpected Gift of Cancer
A Prescription to Taste 'cooking with cancer'
Cajun and Creole Cooking with Miss Edie and The Colonel
A Country Music Christmas
Emergency Preparedness Handbooks
Quick & Easy Holiday Treats with Style
Quick & Easy Entrees with Style
Quick & Easy Salads & Breads with Style
Deborah Ford's "The Grits Guide to Life"
Recipes For Life
All Cooked Up
Precious Family Memories of Elvis
The Presley Family & Friends Cookbook

Coming soon 2010 and beyond

The Sisterhood Ride
Women of True Grit
How to Mop with your Pearls On
Entertaining with Miss Edie and The Colonel
plus a companion book 'My First Tea Etiquette Party' for kids.
ABC of Sales and Sales Etiquette

Stay tuned to www.ediehand.com for book updates,
tours and releases with Edie and Friends

The
Soldier's Ride

A NOVELLA

Inspiration from Desperation

Edie Hand
with Jeffery Addison

Parkway Publishers

Library of Congress Cataloging-in-Publication Data

Hand, Edie, 1951-
The soldier's ride : a novella / by Edie Hand and
Jeffery Addison.
p. cm.
Summary: "The story is a salute to veterans every-
where and the sacrifice they make for our country.
It is also a story for those who are left behind and
the sacrifices they make in wartime"--Provided by
publisher.
ISBN 978-1-933251-67-7
I. Addison, Jeffery, 1947- II. Title.
PS3608.A6985S65 2009
813'.6--dc22
2009018893

Dedicated to those who lay down

their lives to ensure freedom...and

to those who say goodbye as each

soldier begins his ride.

Acknowledgments

Thank you, Edie for allowing me
to accompany you on these wonderful rides.

Jeffery Addison

It has been my distinct honor to write with Jeffery Addison. He brings out the best in me! We both would like to especially thank Sandy Horton for her eyes into the spirit of our 'Ride' books. You are the best editor we have ever worked with to date! Thank you so very much to Wendy Dingwall for believing in The Ride Series and for making it happen with Parkway Publishers.

Any successful venture needs wind beneath its wings to allow what you conceive to believe to be true. My son, Linc Hand has been my partner in dreams of reality. Thank you, Linc, for you are a piece of my strength that comes through these pages.

Karen Waldron is my Hollywood connection who understands the heart of "The Ride Series". Thank you, Karen, for believing and making the efforts that will bring these words to life on the big screen. A very special thank you to Mark Waldron, Jack Hargrove, Ashley Harris and Vicki Rickles for allowing us to use the lyrics from your poignant song "A Miracle In Me" in this book.

By the Grace of God I am here to share 'a miracle in me' with all of you!

Edie Hand

The Bench

She did not notice the car's temperature gauge steadily climbing into the red as she eased impatiently to a stop at the red light. Distracted by the cell phone conversation, she first threatened and then pleaded with the person on the opposite end of the call. She tried not to show her real emotions. That showed weakness and put her in a bad position. However, the deal was quickly going bad and she was bound to save it before she returned to the office.

Lunch was long since forgotten. Her appointment—a banker who represented millions of potential investment dollars—that she kept waiting at the restaurant had understood. He was on the same treadmill. Diana Meade was in full-blown crisis mode. The others who kept calling her, tripping the call waiting on her cell phone, eager to tell her their own problems, would have to stand in line and await their turn.

She was a busy woman. She did not have time to argue with this guy, to try to explain to him the supreme logic of allowing Diana and her venture capital firm to take over his struggling little company. So what if he inherited it from his father and promptly ran it into the ground?

"Look, the company will be profitable again once we get aboard," she explained.

"I still don't know. Some of these people are like family. They have been with us for..."

Profitable even if some of the dead wood will have to be trimmed away to make it so, Diana thought. Her company, the new owners would take no prisoners.

The car's engine abruptly began missing and sputtering, practically ignoring her when she gave it gas. She lurched away from the traffic light. Then she saw the first fingers of steam poking up around the edges of the hood.

"Aw, brother! What the...? No, not you, Sol. The car. I think it's running hot on me or something. And I just had it in the shop last..." She pounded the steering wheel with the palm of her free hand, but not loud enough for the man she was talking with to

suspect that she was losing her cool. "Look, let me go and see if I can drop this thing off at the dealership or something. But remember what I said, Sol. Sometimes you have to make some tough decisions to save a company. Think about all the rest of those jobs that will be lost if you go under. Then you have nothing to show for all the hard years you put in, Sol. Nothing to show."

Now the car seemed completely out of power, weak, the engine sputtering, threatening to stop altogether. She almost willed the dying auto off the street and out of traffic, edging to a jerky stop at what passed for a curb in this unfamiliar section of Nashville. She tried to ignore the angry horn-blowers who did not think she was getting out of the way fast enough. She could not help it. She angrily shook her fist at them as she climbed out of the car, kicking the nearest tire, already dialing the number for AAA.

"It could be an hour or two, Miss Meade," the dispatcher reported. "Sorry. Everybody we have is out. Lots of cars overheating when it..."

The overhead sun bore down; its rays were relentless. A trickle of sweat ran down the back of her neck and disappeared at the collar of her dress suit.

Her makeup would be a fright. Her hair was already falling into her face. She had a three o'clock and a four. She would have to try to re-do everything, if she could only get back to the office.

There were trees on the other side of the street. A row of tall trees and an expanse of grass beyond through some kind of big metal gates.

"Okay, okay. Hurry then," she ordered, fighting her temper and the urge to command the dispatcher to get a wrecker there in five minutes or else deal with Diana Meade. "Hurry! It's stifling out here and I have work to do. I don't have time for this!"

When the light changed, she hurried across the street toward the shade of the trees as quickly as she could in heels. She ignored the catcalls and whistles from some rednecks in a pickup truck. She looked about for a bench where she could sit out of the sun's range and return some calls, answer some text messages, check her e-mail. She may as well take advantage of this delay to get some work done.

Only a dirty, graffiti-laden bus bench with no shade from the relentless sun seemed available. The big, metal gates she had noticed before were open, only twenty feet away, and covered with shade.

Maybe she could find a place to sit down in there.

She walked into what she quickly saw was a huge cemetery. Long rows of identical white crosses, per-fectly aligned, stood planted in the well-groomed grass, their symmetry broken occasionally by statues, benches or towering shade trees. A massive American flag crowned a flagpole just beyond the gate. There did not seem to be anyone around, though. Nothing but crosses.

Diana made for the closest bench beneath one of the bigger trees, one with the deepest, darkest shade, but still within sight of her car so she would see the wrecker when it arrived. Maybe if she tipped the driver a few bucks he would drop her off at the office on the way to the dealership.

The phone chirped as she sat down. When she saw the familiar number on caller ID, she answered immediately.

"Mom, you going to make my game?"

"I don't know, Robbie. The car quit on me out here in the middle of nowhere and I'm waiting for a tow truck."

"Aw, Mom, you said you'd come to our last game, at least. You haven't been to one all year and guess

what. Dad is…"

"Look, I can't help it, Robbie" she snapped. "Maybe if your dad wasn't off somewhere playing soldier he could be of some help…"

Her son was quiet, just as he always was when she used that tone when she mentioned his father. Despite their divorce, Jeff was still supposed to be around doing things dads and ex-husbands did, going to their son's soccer games, jumping to quit whatever he was doing and come rescue her if her car died on a stifling day. His Tennessee National Guard unit had been called up again. He was somewhere in Iraq for almost a year now. When she and their son needed him most, he was on the other side of the world.

She had been ignoring calls from him the last few days. She was mad at her ex. Mad because he was gone. He was the one who shipped out only days after the divorce was final, before she even had time to get used to the idea. He chose a uniform and a gun and some grand and glorious adventure instead of being there to help her. And now he expected her to jump and answer anytime he called?

"Okay, I'll be there, if AAA gets here and tows my

car, honey. And if the dealership has a loaner until
they get mine running again, and if everything at the
office is...

"I love you, Mom. Gotta go. Dad's on the caller
ID."

Sure he was on the phone. But what good was
he from 12,000 miles away? Robbie's soccer game
was south of town, on Franklin Road, nowhere near
Baghdad.

She flipped the phone closed, eased back on the
bench, and tried to find a calm eye in the middle
of this storm she called a life. It was, thankfully,
much cooler in this place than it had been on the
street. Cooler and quieter. She could hardly hear the
whoosh of the traffic on the busy street where her
automobile lay to the side, a casualty of the heat.
Even the cement bench was cool on her legs and wet
back. She idly kicked off her heels and sat there for a
moment, enjoying the feel of the grass on her feet.

When her pulse slowed, she would make the call
to the office to tell Paul Woods that she would be
late getting back, that she needed to disappear for a
little while this afternoon to see her son's last soccer
match of the summer. She rummaged in her purse,

found a tissue, and wiped the sweat from her upper lip and forehead, and then began looking for makeup and lipstick. She knew she must look a fright and she could not let anyone—even a tow-truck driver—see her without the proper makeup.

Then Diana Meade did something she rarely did. She postponed the makeup and allowed herself to relax, to recline against the bench back. She closed her eyes. Something about this peaceful place had taken away the urgency of that next telephone call. Maybe it was the songbird, yodeling away high in the tree above her, or the surprisingly fresh breeze, carrying the smell of new-cut grass and the castanet sounds of distant cicadas. There might even be a storm trying to get itself started off in the sky to the southwest, promising a refreshing breeze.

She would just rest her eyes for a moment, cool off a bit, and she would get back to work on the cell phone. By then, maybe she would be rescued.

"It certainly is a peaceful place, isn't it, Miss?"

The voice next to her was not threatening at all. It did not startle Diana in any way, but she quickly opened her eyes and looked sideways to see who had joined her on the cemetery bench. An old woman now occupied the seat next to her.

Diana had not heard her approach or sit down. Maybe she had been concentrating too much on the soothing sounds of the songbird and the cicadas, or too occupied with her thoughts about the office, Robbie, her ex-husband. The woman who sneaked up on her was easily eighty years old, dressed in clothes more appropriate for a day in January than a steaming-hot one in late May.

The woman did not return Diana's glance. She stared out across the cemetery at the rows of crosses, watching them intently, as if she expected them to rush to formation and begin to march in cadence.

"Sorry. I didn't hear you..." Diana started, primarily to see if the woman knew where she was, that someone else occupied the bench where she had settled down. Sometimes, with old people, it was hard to tell if they had their wits about them. "Look, I don't have any change with me."

The old woman waved her hand as if to say, "Don't worry, Miss, and keep your money. "

"I'm not here to ask for anything. I just hope I didn't frighten you, dear." The old woman now looked at Diana and smiled. Her eyes sparkled and her teeth were even and white. "I don't want to disturb you. Even we heavenly angels sometimes like to sit and rest in a nice shady place. It's especially good for the soul, you know. And you never know what interesting people you might meet out here."

Diana moved, almost imperceptibly, an inch or two farther away from the old woman and her talk of angels. She seemed harmless, though. Not wild-eyed or threatening. Still, you could never be sure when she might start talking in tongues or conjuring up spirits.

"Oh, it's okay. You're really not disturbing me. I have some calls to make, but they can wait a few minutes, I guess. I'm just sitting here, trying to cool off, catch my breath. My car gave up the ghost over there on…"

"Yes, I saw you. Someone's coming to help? Your husband? Maybe a relative or someone?"

Diana pursed her lips and showed the woman her left hand. A ring, but on the wrong finger. Certainly not a wedding ring.

"I'm much too busy anymore for a husband, and even if we were still married, he'd be of no help to me. He is on the other side of the world, acting out some outlandish video game. My son...he's still too young to drive so..." Diana's voice trailed off. She looked at the old lady, still half expecting her to erupt into a fit of some kind. Diana did not want to make any sudden move that might frighten her, set her off as she figured out a way to extricate herself from a conversation with the odd woman. "But I guess I am married. Married to Woods, Meade, and Palmer," Diana said, before she even realized she was speaking aloud again. The woman looked confused, her head turned sideways. "Venture capital. We buy companies with other people's money, cut costs, lay off the employees and off-shore the work so we can build up the cash flow, and then we sell the business to somebody else at a profit and keep a bunch of the money for ourselves. Some people flip burgers. I flip businesses."

"Well. That *is* an interesting way to make a living."

The old woman showed no interest in Diana and her unusual job. With a smile remaining on her lips, she raised her lined face and cocked her gray head, turning an ear to listen to the bird still singing away in the tree above them.

"He certainly seems happy, like he has so much

to sing about that he does not want to miss a note. Reckon he is singing a song for his lady?"

"Could be."

Diana pulled the cell phone from the compartment inside her purse and pressed a button. She studied the long list of missed calls on the phone's display. She was already prioritizing, deciding which ones needed touching first, as soon as she could politely begin ignoring her new bench mate. Normally she would not have worried about being polite in this situation, but something about this lady prevented her from being gruff or impolite.

Diana realized what it was. She reminded her so much of her late grandmother. Granny Foster. Her mother's mother. Diana had spent so many summers at her farm up near the Kentucky border. It was one of the few and fondest childhood memories that she allowed herself to cling to.

"Or maybe he's telling you and me a story, one with a happy ending." The old woman nodded in the direction of the nearest row of white crosses.

"Ma'am, I'm afraid I don't believe in happy endings," Diana said with a snort. "I gave up on those a long time ago.

She could not tell if the woman heard her or not.

"There are not many happy endings in a place like this," she went on. "Did you ever wonder what kind of stories all these folks buried out here could tell if they were still around. Or if they could find somebody who was not too busy to listen?"

Diana kept her eyes on the cell phone's display but raised her eyebrows and shook her head once to signal, "No." She did not take the time to consider if she had just been insulted by this old woman she was allowing to share her shade.

"Why, every one of those crosses out there is a story. Stories as far as the eye can see. Someone had a life cut short, a promise not kept. Someone else lived to a ripe old age, saw the color of his grand-children's hair and heard the sound of their voices singing Christmas carols. That one right there.

Private Josiah Malone
106th Infantry
Born, 1922. Died, Battle of the Bulge,
December 25, 1945.

Private Malone died on Christmas Day. Twenty-two, twenty-three years old. Wonder if he had a wife or girlfriend back home waiting for him to come marching back. How did his mother feel when she got the news? What words did he write in his last letter home to her or his sweetheart? I wonder what stories Mr. Malone would tell us if only he could. What advice he might give us about living a full, rich life if we should be granted the chance he was not."

Diana cleared her throat.

"I try not to dwell on such things, Mrs...."

"Celia. Just call me Celia. But dear, there are so many stories here. Good ones and bad ones, happy ones and sad ones. Stories we can learn from. Some, I bet, that would give us a good chuckle. Some that would inspire if taken in the proper light." Celia turned back to face Diana and smiled broadly, placing her hands in her lap. "That's one of the things angels do, you know. We listen to people's stories then we share them with somebody else if there is a good purpose in it. You don't have to _dwell_ on them. They are right here, all around us. You can't help but hear them if you just take the time to listen and learn from them. Jesus called them parables. You remember the parables from Sunday school?"

Diana forced a smile, still uncharacteristically humoring the old lady, and said, "Well, Celia, I don't have time to listen to anybody's stories...parables... today, and as soon as AAA gets here, I'm back to doing whatever it is that I do to keep food on the table and the wolf away from the door."

But the old lady did not seem to hear Diana's gentle dismissal. She still had that slight smile on her wrinkled face when she reached to touch Diana gently on her arm. Diana avoided flinching or rebuffing the familiar gesture. The old woman, odd as she was with her talk of angels and parables and the compelling stories of long-dead soldiers, still seemed to be harmless.

"Now there, that one. That's a truly remarkable story." Celia pointed with her other hand to an inconspicuous cross, one just like all the others, three rows down and one across. "Christopher Lawrence rests there. At least his body does. Christopher is with Jesus. He was something, a beautiful young man, bluest eyes you ever saw, and a shock of wheat for hair, muscles from working and playing football, and a sharp mind. Sharpest mind you ever saw. And you know what that boy did? He preached his first formal sermon when he was twelve years old.

A sermon about Shadrach, Meshach and Abednego and Daniel and the fiery furnace. He was born with a gift for communication. I bet he could spin us a wonderful tale! He's not here, though, but I know the story. You may recognize parts of it, too."

Try as she might, Diana could not be annoyed with the old lady for interrupting her very busy day. She was clearly lonely, not to be deterred from her mission of talking the ears off anybody she might encounter in the cemetery that day.

It appeared Diana Meade had drawn the short straw.

OK, she decided. I may just as well listen to her story as to somebody on the telephone calling me and my ancestors vile names. Besides, it was surprisingly pleasant there at the edge of the cemetery. Cool, the air clean, the bird's song like lovely background music serving as a gentle soundtrack for the old woman's story. The story that she seemed so doggedly determined to share.

What was the harm in humoring her, listening to her, but only until AAA showed up to tow her car?

She shrugged.

She would allow the old "angel" to tell her tale.

The Ride

The Big Ben alarm clock on his nightstand rang promptly at 4:30 every morning of the week. He kept it far enough from his reach that he was halfway out of bed when he pushed in the pin in the back to shut it off. He could not afford to fall back asleep. He stood, stretched, combed out his shock of wheat straw hair, pulled on his jeans, tee shirt, and sneakers, and then, on his way out, took a big gulp of milk directly from the glass bottle in the icebox. There was no one around to catch him committing this most serious transgression. His parents would not be up for another couple of hours.

By the time Christopher Lawrence was on his bike, heading for the parking lot behind the hardware store ten blocks away, he was awake, alive, and happy to be about his business. The truck waited for him and the rest of the bunch of sleepy-eyed boys on bikes. He filled the canvas bag tied to his handlebars with four dozen rolled-up-and-tied cop-

ies of the Nashville *Tennessean* newspaper. Then he rode through the sleeping neighborhoods, tossing the papers onto front porches or dropping them at the ends of driveways. In the winter, it was so dark he could hardly see his way between the occasional streetlights. Sometimes snow swirled in the circles of illumination or a thick fog made it hard to see, but he still showed up and did what he agreed to do when he took the route.

Nine months out of the year, he ran home after he threw the last newspaper, gobbled up the breakfast his mother always had arrayed on the table for him, and caught the bus for school. In the summer, he ate and then went out the backdoor, down the steps and to the side yard. There he pulled the old, rusty push mower from beneath the porch. He oiled it up, checked the gasoline in the can he carried, and headed off to mow lawns all over the south part of town for a buck apiece. He only stopped to rest during the hottest part of the day. Of course, he still had his chores to do around the house, too.

Chris Lawrence worked so hard because he had a dream. A dream that started with four wheels and an engine. He intended to earn and save enough money to buy himself a ride, a car, and he planned to have enough money saved so he could buy it the day he turned sixteen and secured his license to drive.

"You're going to wear yourself out and make yourself sick," his mother worried. But he kept his almost-perfect grades up and still found time and energy to play baseball with the guys and hang out at the soda shop with his friends. He even found time to help his two younger twin brothers with their homework and their curve balls.

Oh, he may have fallen asleep a time or two during the service, but he never missed church. Often, it was he who brought the message if Reverend Hamilton was away. His devotion and his knowledge of the Bible amazed those who heard him. His talent for communicating what he knew and how it applied to all ages in the congregation made him a powerful preacher already. Everyone loved the fresh approach and the power he brought to his sermons. They knew he would be a powerful minister someday.

"You should be saving that money for college, not some old rattle-trap of a car," his father counseled, but Chris had an answer for that, too. He always seemed to have a plan. The rest of his life was no exception.

"Dad, I'm going to college when I finish high school and I know you can't afford to pay my way," he told him, his deep blue eyes serious, his face showing his determination. "Then I'll go to seminary and learn to preach so I can show people the way. I am going to use the radio to reach people with the message of Jesus. There will be other ways, too, like radio with pictures. It's coming. Think how many people will hear the word! And I plan to marry the prettiest girl in Middle Tennessee and give you the most beautiful grandkids you've ever seen. And it all starts with the ride I'm gonna buy as soon as I turn sixteen."

Chris Lawrence got his faith and zeal from parents who taught him the basics early and from two grandfathers who were ministers. He grew up listening to them explain the Bible and the promise it made to those who listened, learned, and opened their hearts to embrace it.

So he formulated his plan and began following it to the letter before he became a teenager. The car was a big part of it. The ride would give him freedom, a chance to cruise around town with his friends,

meet girls, and have fun, but it would also allow him to get an after-school job farther from home, one that paid more than throwing newspapers and mowing lawns. The money would allow him to learn more about his religion, grow his perspective, learn to lead others to the strong faith he held. If he had not already found the perfect woman by then, he would be on the lookout for one at college. He was confident he would find her, that God would show her to him, and the rest of the plan would play out, just as he intended.

Just as God had told him it would.

His parents only shook their heads and smiled. Theirs was a normal kid in most ways, but smarter and harder working than many. They knew of no others who had such a detailed plan and the strength of mind to follow it. Still, they could not complain. Chris was not perfect, though he caused them little trouble beyond the high-spirited mischief that sometimes found him. Maybe his stubborn streak was a little hard to deal with sometimes, but his parents were thankful. Thankful and proud of their oldest son and what he hoped to do with the rest of his life.

Chris could recite the driver license manual from memory and, of course, passed the test the same day he turned sixteen. With his dad in the passenger seat, he had been expertly guiding the family car around town since he was thirteen, so the driving test was nothing to worry about. And by the weekend after his sixteenth birthday, he had an old Ford automobile towed from a used car lot across town and parked beside the house. He kept busy between summer jobs and church, washing and polishing his car as if the faded paint might actually shine again. With his dad's help, he changed the oil and plugs, tuned the engine, installed new brakes and put on a better set of used tires. Through hard work and more than a little willpower, he got the old Ford running surprisingly smoothly for a vehicle with its mileage and age and history of abuse.

His mother watched out the kitchen window as her two men worked together on the old car. She brought them ice tea and fussed mildly about the mess they were making in her yard, but she could not help but smile as the project approached completion.

Finally, on a Friday afternoon in late September,

with the leaves along Hope Street flaring to full color, Chris pronounced his ride ready to roll. Dad scratched his chin, cocked his head, listened to the engine as Chris cranked it again, and finally agreed with his boy's expert assessment.

"Okay if I take her for a spin tonight, Dad?" he asked.

"Sure. Be careful, though. You got money so you can call home if she breaks down on you?"

"She won't break down, Dad," he said. "She's my ride. She will do just fine."

Chris cleaned up, put on a fresh tee shirt and jeans and a few extra splatters of cologne. He stood for a moment and admired the vehicle, adjusted the side mirrors one more time before he climbed behind the wheel, cranked her up, and slowly backed the car out into the street. He waved to his mom as she sat watching him from the front porch swing, seated next to his dad. He gave the horn a few honks. The sound it made was rough and more of a squawking growl than a toot, but it sounded sweet and resonant from where Chris sat, behind the steering wheel of his ride.

He shifted to first gear, eased out the clutch,

gave it some gas, and steered his dream ride down the street until he disappeared out of sight, around the corner, beyond the houses at the far end of the block where night was quickly claiming territory.

The side yard looked empty now. The street was oddly quiet without the idling and backfiring of the Ford, the voices of father and son as they shouted to be heard over the roar of the unmuffled motor.

There, in the swing on the front porch of the house on Hope Street, Chris Lawrence's mother squeezed her husband's hand tighter. She could not help it. She cried quietly as she watched her boy and his ride disappear, swallowed up by the gathering darkness.

The Train

In December, just over a year after Chris got his ride running and in the middle of his senior year in high school, something happened that in no way fit into his life-plan. The Japanese bombed Pearl Harbor in Hawaii. That event, thousands of miles away and halfway across the Pacific Ocean from Nashville, abruptly changed everything for everyone, including Chris Lawrence.

Many of his classmates who were already seventeen years old (or sixteen and could get their parents to verify a lie about their age) quit school immediately and went down to enlist. Chris's mom and dad persuaded him to wait until he graduated, until he had his diploma so he might get duty that helped win the war through some means other than toting a rifle or riding a submarine.

Someone else influenced his decision, too.

Her name was Marie Benedict. And she was another factor that put a crimp in the master plan

Chris Lawrence had laid out for himself.

He never planned to fall in love until after he completed college. But when he nailed down that part of the plan, he did not yet know Marie Benedict. He met her shortly after he took an after-school job early in his senior year at her dad's radio repair shop in downtown Nashville. Chris drove the store truck to pick up and deliver radios that Mr. Benedict repaired, and Marie, after school, checked them in and out, writing up the trouble tickets on the broken ones and the invoices for those her dad had repaired.

Marie, a senior at another high school, had never met Chris. However, Chris had seen her in the crowd at baseball games when he and his team played her school. She was hard to miss!

Marie Benedict was a beauty, no doubt about it. Her sharp sense of humor and an active mind intimidated most of the boys who considered dating her. Chris soon discovered that she, too, had devised a detailed, long-term plan. Hers did not include seriously dating anyone either, not until she had graduated college and earned her teaching certificate. Then—and only then—she would begin looking for the perfect man to be the father of the brood of children she intended to raise. By "raise" she meant bringing them up in the church, teaching them to speak at least three languages, encouraging them to become adept in mathematics and science, and making certain that they were well versed in great literature and philosophy. And by "perfect man" she meant someone who would love her unconditionally but would also understand her beliefs and devotion to the church.

By December of 1941, they were not only dating seriously but they were also altering their schematics to work each other into their long-term plans. Chris could still go to college, then seminary. Marie would go to college, too, while Chris was away in seminary. They would marry and be together when finances and time permitted, and they would both be practical enough to know when that was.

Only then, after all that had been accomplished, would they begin the family they both wanted. They had mapped out their ride through life together, and they both agreed on the route it would take.

Then history intervened.

Like his parents, Marie advocated that Chris finish high school before he did anything else. He reluctantly agreed, even as he watched his friends ride out of town, one after the other, on the troop trains that pulled away almost daily from Union Station.

As winter faded, the handsome young couple spent evenings after work parked near the lake in Centennial Park. War and battles and death seemed impossible to imagine there, even if the newspapers and radio broadcasts and newsreels at the movie theaters were full of it. Their positive words could not keep the worry from their faces as they wondered if all they had forecasted for themselves was about to veer hard left, out of their control. As they sat on the hood of the Ford and fed the ducks and swans at the park lake, they made promises to each other that they fervently hoped—and fully intended—to be able to keep.

"You know I'll be back soon," Chris told her. "This war won't last long. I probably won't even get overseas before Hitler gives up and Japan throws in the towel."

"From your lips to God's ear," she said, not convinced. "Have you decided where you are going to enlist?"

"I think so. The Marines need radio repairmen according to the recruiter. It would be a good trade for me to fall back on someday if I ever needed to, and you know that I want to own radio stations someday, maybe a whole network, so I can preach God's word to as many people as I can."

"Does the enemy throw grenades at radio repair-men?" she asked with a humorless smile.

"If they're smart, they do. Radio's broke, the whole platoon is in trouble. It is, you know, the most important job in the entire war."

He winked. She threw a handful of sesame seeds at him, then put her arm around him and brushed the seeds from his hair and off his shirt. She rested her head on his shoulder and kissed him lightly on the cheek.

"Promise me you will come back, Christopher Lawrence. Promise me that. And that you will still want to marry me and spend the rest of your life with me and raise that big family we both want. That's all I ask."

He turned to look at her. In the glow from the setting sun, her face was radiant, beautiful, but he did not miss the tear that ran down her cheek.

"I promise. You know I promise. And you promise me you will be waiting for me. We got kids to bring up speaking Latin and quoting Shakespeare and doing square roots in their pretty little blonde heads."

"I promise. I love you. I'll wait. Just come on back to me in one piece as quick as you can."

"I promise." He should have left it there, but something else nagged at him. "But, Marie, if something should happen to me, whether I don't come back, or I come back...well, not the same...promise me that you will..."

She put her fingers to his lips. Then she moved them aside so that she could kiss him, holding her lips on his until she knew he would not try again to extract from her that particular kind of promise.

"Hush. You just come back. Win the war. Then come back to me. I never intended to fall in love with anybody until I was older and settled and teaching. Then you had to come along and mess all that up. You are not getting out of it now just because the world has gone crazy and they need soldiers to fix it. Hear me?"

"Okay, but still..." He did not try to finish the

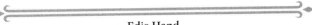

sentence. He just kissed her again and pulled her as close as he could without both of them tumbling off the hood of his car.

They never seriously considered getting married before he shipped out. They did discuss it, just as they did everything else in their planned future. The future was so uncertain, the news they were hearing on the radio so overwhelmingly bad. They never said it aloud but neither wanted to tie the other to something that might not last. There would be plenty of time, they told each other, if it was God's will, for them to marry.

Chris Lawrence enlisted in the Marines and almost immediately received orders to ship out for boot camp two days after a subdued high school graduation ceremony. On a warm, bright spring day, his mother and father and his girlfriend took him and his single cardboard suitcase down to Union Station, a few blocks from downtown Nashville. His dad and he shook hands and avoided looking at each other. His mother and Marie seemed to be leaning on each other, holding each other upright, trying to keep a sunny look on their faces for his benefit even as they drew strength from each other.

"I'll write every day," he promised them. "Maybe twice on Saturdays if the Japs will give me time."

No one laughed at his feeble joke.

"Just remember your promise," Marie said.

"Uh, which one was that?" She reached to cuff him on the shoulder but he grabbed her arm and pulled her close to him in a tight embrace. "I love you, Marie. I will be back and we will follow that plan of ours. You can take that to the bank. Pray for me. Pray for all of us, okay?"

"I will," she promised. "You know I will. And here's something I want you to keep with you."

She handed him a small, smooth stone. It was a deep red color with streaks of tan.

"What is this?"

"It is a courage stone. My grandmother was Cherokee. She gave me several when I was a little girl. 'Anytime you need courage, pray to God and touch this stone,' she told me. The Indians considered them a symbol of faith, of trusting in a power that is unseen but powerful. You need one now, Christopher. Between God, me, your folks, and the courage stone, you will come back to us."

Chris kissed her, hugged his mother, shook his

dad's hand, and then stepped back and saluted. He turned and fell into the line of young men who walked briskly down the steps to the train cars lined up for them on the tracks beneath the station. Few of them looked back. Bound for an uncertain fate, they did not want to look at their families and sweethearts again—they might turn and run back to them if they did.

Once Chris was in his railcar, seated, he looked out the window, trying to see beyond the railing on the observation deck above. He spotted the three of them, still standing there, silhouetted by the afternoon sun, looking for his face at the train's windows. He waved and got their attention just as the cars began to lurch forward, squeaking and clanking.

They waved back, but he was too far away and the sun was too bright for him to see their faces clearly. Too far away to see the tears on the faces of his mother and wife-to-be as they watched the man they loved go away to war.

He was no longer just a son or a fiancé. He was taking his first ride as a soldier.

Marie Benedict stood at the railing, looking for him, wondering what God had in store for him, for them. Whatever happened, she knew He would give her strength to handle it. Chris was no longer just her fiancé, his parents' son. He was something else. He was a soldier, riding off to do his duty for something right. Brutal, horrible, awful, but right. God had picked him to join the others to correct a wrong, and that was why he was riding away from them on that troop train that day.

Through her tears, Marie prayed that he would soon ride back to them, well and whole and ready to live the idyllic life he and she had planned for themselves. She rubbed her own courage stone. She knew she needed it. At that moment, she understood more clearly than ever why her grandmother gave it to her. She needed faith to believe that Chris would be all right, that he would come back to her with God's help.

She felt the warm smoothness of her grandmother's Cherokee courage stone as she prayed harder than she had ever prayed in her life.

The Homecoming

The bird on the tree branch above the two of them had stopped singing, as if it, too, was listening attentively to the old woman's story. Diana suddenly realized she had been lost in the familiar but powerful tale of young lovers separated by war. She had completely forgotten the phone and its list of digital distractions. She had missed several calls. The caller ID said it was Jeff, her ex-husband, calling.

Oddly, it was the number for his old cell phone, the one he left with his parents when he shipped out. It was not the barracks phone he usually used when he tried to reach her from the other side of the world.

Diana glanced quickly to where she could see her car, still at the side of the road. There was no tow truck in sight.

"Theirs was not an unusual story," Celia said, again touching Diana's arm. "War is hungry for young people. Young people with dreams and plans that don't include guns and blood and death. Since God placed us on this earth, they have answered the call. 'There will always be wars and rumors of war.' Men march off to defend their countries. Women stay behind. Not anymore, of course. Women fight wars, too, for all the same reasons. Duty—rightly or wrongly placed—interrupts those dreams, sometimes temporarily. Sometimes brutally and permanently."

There were tears in Celia's eyes. She wiped them away with the sleeves of her sweater, and then stood and walked over to the cross with Christopher Lawrence's name on it. She touched it gently. Diana watched her for a moment, afraid she might simply wander off and not complete the story. Then Diana remembered something.

"You know, Celia, I once had a courage stone. It belonged to my dad. My mom gave it to me when Jeff and I married. She said to keep it handy because you never know when you might need a little extra spark of courage. I gave one to Jeff, too, the first time he was deployed. I've lost mine somewhere."

"Your mother is right. You never know."

Diana strained to hear Celia's words above the

distant hiss of traffic as she lingered near the cross. Celia returned to the bench and sat next to Diana as she continued her story. Diana's phone buzzed again but she continued to ignore it.

With her true love gone, Marie Benedict tried to keep her same schedule each day. The same one that she had followed since she first fell in love with Chris Lawrence and dedicated her life to being with him. She awoke early and stood at her window, the dormer window facing west toward where Chris now was. Not just on the other side of town, like before, but halfway around the world on some tiny island in the South Pacific. She prayed as fervently as she had ever prayed in her life that God would pro-tect him and send him safely home to her. They had children to birth, a ministry to start, a life together to resume.

She helped her mother with breakfast and drove Chris's car to her dad's radio shop downtown. The car was a part of him she could keep close to her. Work kept her busy but she snatched quick minutes to scan the morning paper for news of how the war was going. She tried to catch the radio network news while she ate her sandwich at lunch, hoping to hear

any bit of good news. It all seemed so nebulous, so inexact and, all too often, bad. It was difficult to get a read on anything.

For a while, there was a letter every other day or so from Chris, from basic training somewhere in California…so very far away…from radio school in Texas, a thousand miles closer, but it may as well have been from another planet in the solar system. For a while, there was hope he would get home for a few days before he shipped overseas, but that soon faded. Then the letters were fewer and farther apart, but longer and more emotional. The slight scrawl in his normally precise penmanship told Marie that he wrote them hurriedly. It was as if he wanted to get all the words out before he decided not to write them at all.

She knew him well enough to know that he was concerned but willing to do what had to be done. He was putting on a brave face, happy to do something to help the cause. She could tell, too, that he was worried about her and what she was doing. Worrying about her worrying about him. That was so much like him.

The last letter she received was mailed from Pearl

Harbor, Hawaii. The postmark on the envelope still sent shivers over her. That place, that infamous day, still resonated powerfully.

The envelope was heavy, eight pages of lined notebook paper, filled with news, thoughts, wishes, "I love yous," a couple of photos of him at the beach, and more. He asked how the car was running and reminded her to use the best grade of motor oil so the cylinders would not get pitted, to check the air in the tires so they were properly inflated.

"I cannot tell you when or where, but I suspect we will ship out soon. We are a good group, great guys from all over the place. One, Tommy Davis, is from Franklin, and he knows some of our friends. I showed him your picture and he kids me and says there will be a kidnapping when we get home. He says a thug like me does not deserve you. I agree but I can't let him get away with saying it, can I? I short-sheeted his bunk three nights in a row and feel I still owe him some more punishment."

She could tell he tried to keep it light and he mentioned God's will several times. However, the final page of his long letter, decorated with Xs for kisses, had a single sentence tacked on as a PS just

below his signature.

"If something should happen to me or if I come back and I am not the same, promise me you will move on and have the happiness you deserve."

She fussed at him in the letter she wrote back, encouraging him, telling him to stop talking about "if" this and "if" that, and that God would protect him. She had no way of knowing if he ever received it. There were no more letters from him.

Marie was listening to the network news on the radio at lunch, horrified by the dramatic reports from London. The sounds of bombs and air raid sirens were clear in the background as the deep-voiced reporter described what he was seeing in the dark streets as the enemy pounded the country. It brought the war home even more powerfully than the photos in the newspaper or the grainy newsreels.

That was when the telephone rang.

"Radio shop."

"Marie? It's Sue Lawrence. Chris's mother."

The voice was unusually formal. Marie usually called her "Mom." Her own mother was "Momma." She and the Lawrences kept in touch. She went over for dinner many times and they sat on the porch and talked for hours each time. Now, Mrs. Lawrence's voice sounded odd, and it was as if they hardly knew each other.

Marie blurted out the first thing that came to mind.

"Is Chris okay?"

There was a pause, a long sigh. Now the voice was shaky.

"We don't know, honey. They just left. Some Marines. They said he had been hurt. It was bad, but they understood he would live. They're bringing him to a hospital in Washington, DC, if...when he's able to travel. Maybe in two or three weeks or maybe as long as a couple of months. We're going, of course, whenever it is. Do you want to..."

"Yes! Please let me know what else you hear, okay? Please."

Mrs. Lawrence said something else, something about how they said he was hurt doing something heroic, but the buzzing in Marie's ears was too loud to hear anything else. After she hung up the telephone, she sat there for a full fifteen minutes, ignoring the blaring phone that tried to interrupt her thoughts.

She prayed. She rationalized. He was alive. That was the important part. She prayed some more. But how hurt was he? How badly injured? What would be left of the Chris she loved so much?

They left Nashville in Mr. Lawrence's car on a cold, foggy February morning, the wheels spinning ominously on the black skim ice that coated the bridges outside of town. Snow fell heavily and it was almost midnight-dark at mid-day as they made their way through the Shenandoah Valley and across Virginia. They could hardly see the Capitol building and the Washington Monument through the snow showers as they skirted Arlington Cemetery at dusk and tried to find the route to the military hospital. They still knew little about Chris, his injuries, how it happened. They only knew that he was still bed-ridden, that he would need long therapy to recover from his wounds.

Once in the military hospital, they found their way to Chris's ward, but a nurse still had to lead them to him. Even then, they could not be certain that it was Chris on that narrow bed, a single sheet pulled to his chin and a green blanket over his legs. He was just one among many in a ward filled with beds, at least a hundred of them. Each held a man, and they all exhibited a wide array of bodily damage, from a simple cast on some to others who were wrapped mummy-like in blood-soaked bandages, tubes draped over them.

Many missed limbs. Others were horribly burned or otherwise scarred. Some slept. Others groaned in pain. Still others read or talked happily with visitors.

Chris was lying on his back, his face wrapped in bandages from his upper lip to the top of his head. His dad, his mother, and Marie stood there next to the bed for a moment. Each of them allowed their eyes to veer downward, checking to see that his arms and legs were all still there.

The nurse who led them to his bed asked, "Did they tell you about his wounds? No?" Her voice dropped to a whisper. "I wish they would do a better job of that. He has lost his eyesight. He's blind."

"You mean temporarily?" his father asked.

The nurse shook her head, "No."

The three visitors looked at each other. Marie and Mrs. Lawrence once again relied on each other for support. Mr. Lawrence chewed his lower lip and studied the worn dress hat that he held in his hands as if he had never seen it before. The nurse waved for them to gather around the bed, closer to her patient, so she could announce their presence to him.

"Corporal Lawrence, you have visitors. You awake?" the nurse asked, nudging his shoulder with her clipboard. "He's one of the quiet ones," she said. "Hard to tell if he's awake or asleep sometimes."

"I asked for no visitors," he said, his voice blurred, maybe from sleep, maybe from the drugs.

"Chris, it's Mom and Dad," Sue Lawrence said, His mother touched his shoulder. "And Marie. Marie came up here with us to see you."

"How are you, Son?" his father asked, willing his voice not to crack.

Marie stood back, allowing them to go first.

"I didn't want you to see me like this." His voice was a hoarse croak. "Maybe later. Maybe…"

"Don't be silly. We're just glad you are okay…" his mother started, but he turned his head away.

"I'll never be 'okay' again, Mom. What good am I? Tell me that. What good am I? I'm blind. I'll never see again. I'm going to be nothing but a burden to you all. I wish one of those shells had…"

He stopped then. They all stood staring at him, at each other, until the nurse gently pushed them out into the aisle, away from his bed. That wounded soldier in that bed could not be their son, her fiancé. He sounded nothing like the Chris they loved so much.

"Lots of them react this way for awhile," she told them. "They feel guilty because they lived and their buddies died. Or they worry about how their family and wives will react when they realize that the man who left will never be the same for the rest of his life." She shooed them on down the aisle. "Look, folks, the chaplain wants to visit with you for a few minutes, and then you should go get dinner, get a good night's sleep. I know the drive up here was difficult, the weather, not knowing what you would find when you got here. Why don't you all plan on coming back tomorrow? Then you can start helping him get better. It is going to take a lot in his case, but something tells me you folks will get it done."

The chaplain prayed with them and told them what little he knew. Chris had been manning a radio at a forward post so they could call in an artillery strike on an enemy position. They came under

a heavy barrage. One of the shells exploded right in front of him, wounding him badly. Other shells landed nearby. Three soldiers died instantly. Three others were badly hurt. Chris's eyes were damaged and he lost a lot of blood but he did not give up. He knew he and his radio were the only hope the survivors had.

"Your boy did a very brave thing," the chaplain said. "Even as badly as he was hurt, he somehow found the right buttons and dials on the radio and transmitted a call for help. He was on the verge of blacking out, but he could hear the other boys and tell they were in bad shape. He stayed conscious long enough to guide the medics to the foxhole. He saved those other three boys. No doubt about it. Terrible as he was hurt, he saved the other boys."

"Father, he seems so..." Marie started.

"I know. He'll have to learn to deal with his blindness. That may be the easy part. He seems like a headstrong young man and he has made up his mind that he is no good to anybody anymore. I'll do what I can. I'll pray for him. Pray with him. I suggest you do the same."

"We will. He's back. He's alive," Marie said. "That's

what really matters. God will make us strong, make him strong."

The chaplain rubbed his forehead and pursed his lips.

"I hope so. But there is one thing that you should know. Your young man has given up on God. And he is convinced that God has given up on him."

The three of them looked at each other, then embraced in a three-way hug. And each of them said a silent, fervent prayer.

The Porch

It was two months before they brought Chris home. A facility right there in Nashville could teach him how to do the everyday things—how to shave, brush his teeth, how to find his way around in a dark world. Chris, hardly an eager student, learned quickly, as he always had. By the time his other wounds had healed completely, he could function and manage for himself with little help.

He informed everyone that he wanted none.

He pointedly refused to allow his mother to do things for him that he could do for himself. That included many tasks she had always done for him before. Things like folding his clothes and putting them neatly in the dresser in his room.

"Just because I'm blind as a bat doesn't mean I can't fold a pair of drawers." He spoke in monotone—no anger, just a sad sort of hopeless resignation.

When Marie was around, he remained mostly quiet, answering her questions politely but saying

little more, as if she was someone he hardly knew. His mom and dad left them alone on the front porch or in the parlor, but he still refused to do little more than acknowledge her presence. If she mentioned getting married or their plan for their lives, he went stony silent.

He was never short or irritable or angry with her. Worse, he simply ignored her.

After he came home to Nashville, Marie gave him a few months to get his bearings. Finally on a warm July evening, she decided to force the issue. If it hurt his feelings or made him mad, then so be it. She was determined to get beyond his malaise.

Chris sat in the porch swing by himself, she in the wicker chair nearby. His parents had walked to church for the evening.

As usual, Chris seemed to go out of his way to avoid being near her, to keep from even touching her. When she gave him a hug, he pointedly did not return it. Her kiss on his cheek was ignored as if he felt nothing. Though it broke her heart, she decided to wait until he was ready for her touch, to not take it personally, and she hoped God would give her the strength to manage it.

Fireflies dotted the elm trees along the street. The smell of sweet barbecue smoke drifted through the air from a neighbor's outdoor grill. The slight breeze kept at bay what was left of the day's heat.

The two of them had said only a few words to each other since his parents left for church. Then they were quiet for a good fifteen minutes. The only sound—the squeaking of the porch swing's chain as he rocked gently. And the crickets. Few cars passed by. Somewhere in the neighborhood, someone switched on a radio. They could just hear the soft dance music, borne by the breeze. A song they both liked, a song they had once danced to.

"Don't you think it's time we talked, Chris?" she finally asked him.

"How do you think the Cardinals will do this year?" he responded immediately. "Reckon they will have the pitching to take the National League pennant? They should, don't you think?"

She ignored his deflection—his trick anytime anybody brought up his injuries, his experiences in battle, his future. It had grown to be quite maddening for her.

"Let's talk about us. Our plans. There's no reason

we can't still…"

"Musial could hit .400, you know. If Mort Cooper can get another twenty wins this season then there's no reason they can't…"

"Stop it, Chris! You owe it to me—to me and your parents and everybody else who loves you—to listen to me," she said, as forcefully as she had ever spoken to anyone in her life.

Chris heard something in her voice, an exasperated edge he had never heard before. He stopped rocking the porch swing, his face still frozen, his eyes hidden by the dark lenses of his glasses. Even in the dim light from inside the house, she could see a slight tightening of his jaw as if he was steeling himself for an assault of some kind.

Well, you are, she thought. Get ready because here it comes, Mr. Christopher Lawrence.

"Okay. Say what you want to say," he told her, but there was no emotion there whatsoever.

She had rehearsed the speech for weeks but now she hardly knew where to begin. She wanted to ask about their marriage plans, school, kids, and more, but she started with his state of mind. Nothing else seemed approachable until they got that out of the way.

She leaned forward, her face barely inches from his, and spoke in a voice just above a whisper.

"They told us at the hospital that you had given up on God. Since you got home, you refuse to go to church with any of us. You refuse to talk with the preacher when he comes over to see you, to pray with you. Chris, what about the plans we had for a radio ministry. What about reaching people with the Word?"

He swallowed hard and adjusted his dark glasses on his nose. He never took them off except to sleep or bathe. He told his father that he wore them all the time because he did not want anyone to see his "dead eyes."

"You tell me, Marie. What kind of God allows the awful things that I saw out there to happen? What kind of God allows men to slaughter other men like that? To cripple and maim and kill others like that? What kind of God does something like this to somebody who had a life plan to serve Him, to carry His word to as many people as he could reach?" He pointed to his eyes. "I was willing to dedicate my life to serving Him and what does He do? He takes away my eyes. He slaps me down before I even get started."

His voice grew strained and there was a near-sneer on his face. "So tell me, Marie. Why should I even consider acknowledging a God who does things like that, much less lift a finger to serve Him? And even if I wanted to, what could I do? Fall down the steps for the Lord? Run smack into a tree in His name? That is not very evangelical, Marie. What does that tell sinners about God and His mercy?"

Marie leaned back in her wicker chair and closed her eyes. She had never heard anyone—much less Chris—speak that way, uttering such words of hopelessness.

"That sounds like a very selfish outlook to me." She swallowed hard. It felt to her as if she had just slapped the man she loved across the face.

"So you are saying that losing my eyes and becoming a cripple, being nothing else but a burden on everybody around me—that if this somehow upsets me then that's just me being old selfish Christopher?""

He snorted and laughed drily.

"Chris, don't you remember? You heard a loud, clear call to preach the gospel. You dedicated your life to heeding that call, and you vowed to do whatever it took to make it happen. You had the whole ride mapped out. Now, just like that, you're going to allow a bump in the road to knock you off course?"

He snorted again, louder, laughed without humor, and slapped his knee.

"A bump in the road! That's a real hoot! I'm blind, in case you haven't noticed. That is one big bump in my book. I can't see a thing, Marie. I can't see your beautiful face, your eyes, your smile. I'll never see the faces of my children. I'll never read a book or catch a baseball or watch a sunset again. I'm at the mercy of whoever has the time to take care of me for the rest of my life. Thank you, God! Thank you for the way you've treated this humble servant! And you can take your word and your plan for me and go straight to..."

"Chris! Listen to yourself," she interrupted, her voice rising to shut off his bitter words. "From the day you decided to preach, you had it easy. I know you worked hard to get your car and to get your journey started, but it was easy for you. You are smart. You read things and you comprehend them immediately. You can form your ideas and communicate them to others so they understand, too. Lots of people who want to tell others about God and His plan for our salvation don't have that ability. You live in the United States of America where the founders put it right there in the Constitution that we can practice our religion as we see fit. Think of the millions of people in the world who don't have that privilege. You have parents who love you and never once mocked your beliefs or your plans. Think about those who want to follow Christ but have no one to support them in their walk."

She leaned forward to touch his knee. He did not draw back but turned his face away from her, toward the empty street and the black, dark night.

"Life is a bumpy road, Chris. Bumpy and full of curves. We rarely know what lies beyond that next bend. Sometimes it's happy and glorious. Sometimes it's horrible and tragic. But no matter what awaits us, we either gain strength from it or we allow it to conquer us. "

She put her fingers to his cheek. A few scars were still visible there and she could feel them with her fingertips. He lifted his hand from his lap. She half expected him to slap her hand away, to suddenly stand and find his way inside, away from her, but he did not. He rubbed his forehead with his own fingers. She took that as a sign that she was getting through to him on some level.

She pressed on.

"Did it ever occur to you that this was a crucial part of God's plan for you, Mr. Christopher Lawrence? How could you minister to people who are hurting if you never experienced hurt in your life? Are you a more effective preacher if you have overcome adversity yourself? Think of the people who are lame or hurting who might draw inspiration from how you have overcome your own adversity. Just think of the platform that gives you, Chris. Just think! We are not supposed to question God's plan. You know that. We talked about it sitting on the hood of your car, feeding the ducks at Centennial Park. We are supposed to have faith that He has a plan for us, and then we are supposed to obediently follow it."

She put her hand on his shoulder.

"If God is testing you, Chris, you are failing, and you have never failed at anything in your life. Not even out there on that island. You were able to save those men's lives. That was a triumph, even if you don't think so. I bet they certainly do!

"I still believe God has big plans for us, for you, Chris. That you are an even stronger vessel than you were before this all happened. God did not send you to war just to defend your country. He made you a soldier for a number of reasons. Yes, to protect us and our country and what we stand for. But he also had you in that place to save the lives of those three other men in that foxhole that day. Now I feel like He is using me to somehow show you that the road ahead may be bumpy but it certainly is not closed. You have hit one enormous roadblock, darling. However, if you are strong enough to overcome it, you will be strong enough to do good for millions of souls who need you and your message. If not, if you take the easier fork in the road, the way of self-pity and surrender, you will have missed your calling and ignored God's plan for you. But I warn you, I'm not going to give up easy."

His face was a blur in the dim light that spilled out from inside the house. The radio down the street somewhere still played a fast number. The crickets seemed to sing along with the music.

She moved to the swing next to him, and then she put her arms around him and pulled him close in a hug. She could not tell for sure but she thought he returned it weakly before his body stiffened. Still she kissed him on one cheek and touched him again with her fingertips on the other.

He kept his face turned away from her, his jaw still set, giving her no sign at all that her words made sense to him.

Just then, Marie could see his parents in the glow of the streetlight at the corner, walking toward them, holding hands like teenagers.

"Think about what I am saying, Chris. Know that I am with you, either way you go on the road ahead. I love you. Your mom and dad love you. Those men you saved that day love you. God loves you. Between all of us, we'll get you back on your life's ride."

He did not say anything in response.

She pulled away from him and stood there for a moment, watching for any sign she had reached him. She went down the steps to meet his parents, to tell them good night, and head on home. She had to be at her dad's radio shop early the next day. She did not tell them of the talk she and Chris had. No, she would wait and see if any of it got through the wall of stubbornness he had erected.

As she climbed into Chris's car, his dream ride, she looked back toward the house where his parents were walking up the steps, greeting their son.

Christopher Lawrence still sat there in the darkness, alone in the porch swing, his face turned away from them.

The dance music from the neighbor's radio had stopped. She heard a familiar melody. She rolled down the car window and listened.

The voices of a choir began to sing in close, perfect harmony. She immediately recognized the words.

"Mine eyes have seen the glory of the coming of the Lord…"

The Second Angel

When the old woman paused in her story, Diana Meade stood suddenly and walked directly to Chris's grave marker, leaving the old storyteller at the bench. The inscription on the cross read, "Cpl. C.W. Lawrence, b. June 21, 1924 – d. December 25, 2004, Bronze Star WWII."

"Christopher W. Lawrence. Does the W stand for…?" she started to ask Celia, but when she looked around, no one was there.

Diana was confused. Maybe she had dreamed the whole thing. Celia, angel or not, was gone. There was nobody in sight in any direction, only the whir of traffic beyond the stone fence and trees that rimmed the cemetery, her broken car still sitting there against the curb, a blazing sun overhead. No tow truck yet.

Her cell phone beeped a distinctive ring tone, signaling a voice mail message. She smiled. Her ringer was a snippet of "Go Rest High on that Mountain," a lovely, inspirational song by country singer Vince Gill. The few notes of music reminded her of the last remnant of a plan she and her Jeff had once had. A plan for a special foundation to help get medical care for sick and injured children who could not afford it. It started when Robbie was diagnosed with a rare blood disorder, but he went into remission, she got busy with the firm, Jeff had his law practice and weekends with the Guard and the grand idea quickly faded away.

Diana checked the time on the screen of her phone. She shook her head. The phone indicated that only five minutes had passed since she first sat down on the cemetery bench to literally cool her heels.

So the old woman and her story had been a dream—just the result of a quick catnap. Diana must have been more tired than she thought. The woman's story had certainly taken an hour so far to tell. Apparently, dreams spun out much faster than angel tales.

She ignored the voice mail and re-dialed AAA. A truck had been scheduled. Everybody's radiators

Edie Hand

were overheating. It was a busy day. Days like this and cold winter mornings were the worst, you know. It might be another hour or two. She clenched her jaws, shutting off the torrent of anger she wanted to unleash on the person on the other end of the telephone.

No point. Wouldn't do any good. The guy might even move her call to the bottom of the stack if she let him have it.

Diana Meade had an odd feeling then. She almost wished the old woman on the bench had been real, not just an exhausted woman's dream. If her suspicions about Christopher Lawrence were true, she would have liked to know what happened next in the story, how it came out. She rarely slept well enough to dream anymore, so, she supposed, she would never know how Christopher and Marie and their plans played out.

Still, there was that name on the tombstone, Christopher W. Lawrence. Could the W possibly stand for...?

"Ma'am, would you have the time?"

She jumped, startled. A man's voice behind her, too close. She turned quickly, ready to fend off an

77

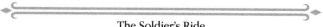

attacker with a well-placed kick, to tell a freeloader to go get a job and leave a stranded businesswoman alone.

He was a slim old man in overalls and work shirt, his eyes hidden by the shadow of his baseball cap brim that was pulled low over his face. He was leaning on a leaf rake and seemed to pose no threat to her.

"Sorry to frighten you, ma'am. I was just wondering if you had the time. Time don't mean much to me anymore but I still ask for it if I want to start a conversation with somebody. Better approach than, 'Hey, lady, let me pick up Celia's story!'" He laughed deeply at whatever joke he had just told himself.

"No, I'm fine," she said. It was Diana's way of not allowing him to think he had gotten the better of her or surprised her in any way. That would be a sign of weakness, of not being prepared for whatever might come at her, even if it was unexpected. Never let them see you sweat. Not in business. Not in relationships. Not in the middle of a military cemetery when surprised by a strange old man leaning on a leaf rake. "I'm waiting for someone to come get my car any minute now," she added with a nod toward

the street, just beyond the cemetery gate, to let him
know she did not anticipate being alone for long.
"What happened to the lady…Celia…though? She
was telling me…"

"Yes'm," he interrupted with a nod that instantly
told Diana that this old fellow was aware of far more
about her and her plight and the conversation with
Celia than she thought. "I was about to take a break
from all this leaf-herdin' and have a seat over there
on that bench and eat my baloney sandwich. You
want to join me?"

"Well, the tow truck should be along any minute
and I should probably go over near my car so…"

She calculated her chances of hailing a taxi and
how long it would take to get one here by phone.

"You don't need to eat any of it unless you want
to," he said with a grin. "Besides, I may just have an
important part of that story you was so wrapped up
in with Celia a few minutes ago."

"Excuse me."

"Me and Celia like to tag-team, just like they used
to do on the wrestling on TV on Saturday nights.
She gets the first part of the story going and then old
Claude comes in and tells some more of it, sorta like

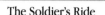

Stan Musial battin' cleanup for the Cards with the bases loaded. I know you want to hear about how Chris and Marie's ride turned out. It's a real good 'un, ma'am. A real good 'un."

Diana Meade looked quickly at her phone, as if it might magically transport her out of this place. Missed calls from Jeff's phone lined up across the screen. She could not imagine why his parents were so insistent on talking to her. They usually only called anymore when they were arranging to pick up Robbie for a visit. Maybe she had forgotten to give them the details of her son's next stay with them. Later. She had other problems at the moment.

The old fellow with the leaf rake still seemed harmless. He was slight enough and had enough years on him she was sure her limited karate skills could keep him at bay if she needed to flee.

Truth was, she had, indeed, become interested in hearing the rest of story, though she had no idea who this man was or how he was connected to Celia. Or if he was just the next act in her suddenly very active dream world.

Maybe, she thought, she should drop by Dr. Moeller's, get something so she could sleep better at night. The pressure of work. Not having her husband home since the divorce. Not even being able to talk to him or depend on him since he went off to live out his macho fantasies and play war. No wonder she tossed and turned at night. Or fell asleep and dreamed strange dreams while sitting on a bench under a tree in the middle of a bunch of dead people.

"OK," she said, and stepped back into the deep shade, easing down on the far end of the bench. Claude leaned his rake against the big tree's trunk and sat on the other end. He made an elaborate ceremony of taking a sandwich wrapped in thick old-fashioned waxed paper from the bib of his overalls, but he did not unwrap it. He placed it on the bench between them and clasped his hands beneath his chin as if he was about to say grace over it.

"You see, Chris was about as far down as a man could go after he got hurt. He had given up on those who loved him, figurin' they were just acting out of pity. He refused to meet with the men from the Marines when they came to tell him that he was going to be awarded the Bronze Star for what he did in that foxhole that day. You know he saved the lives

of three of his brothers-in-arms. He had the idea the Marines were just doing that to sell war bonds or to get him to make speeches or go around trying to improve morale or something. Using him, he said. 'Feel sorry for the blind man. Buy war bonds,' he mocked.

"But mostly he was mad at God. The things Marie told him on the front porch that night touched a nerve. She did more good with that little speech than she knew at the time. He could not get the words out of his head. Especially the part about God testing him and him failing.

Yet Marie Benedict had not fully changed his mind. Christopher W. Lawrence was still one bitter young man and on the top of his blame list for everything that happened was the Lord.

"But he had not counted on the will of some very powerful forces in his life. Marie, of course. She loved Chris. She decided she could be just as stubborn as he could. She was not about to stop trying until she got him back on the ride through life that he and she had started together. Too much was riding on it.

His fellow soldiers would play a part. And, of course, his God. They were all about to shine some

light on that young man's soul, I'm here to tell you. And when they did, whoooeee! Something powerful happened, Miss Meade. Something mighty, mighty powerful!"

Almost as if on cue, a potent shaft of sunlight broke through the thick branches of the huge tree under which the two of them sat. It shone right on the simple cross marker at Christopher Lawrence's grave. The marble glistened and gleamed.

It would not have surprised Diana at all if an angelic choir suddenly began singing. "The Battle Hymn of the Republic." But only the songs of the birds and the ever-present automobile noise hummed away in a constant background drone.

That and the words of the old man, Claude, as he continued the tale of this soldier's ride.

The Foxhole

Marie tried her best to make the books balance. Her father could wire up resistors and capacitors without a schematic and bring back to life a silent, broken radio, but simple debits and credits baffled him. She had already postponed any thoughts of going to college. Her father needed her and he knew it, so he paid her what he could afford to help him out at the shop. He told her that now that the war was over, he could probably find someone part time to do the books. Somebody else needed her, too. Her fiancé, but Chris was not aware of it. At least not yet. He would be. Someday, somehow, he would realize she was not going to give up on him.

Her mind was still on the books and invoices as she answered the jangling telephone. She was surprised to hear Mrs. Lawrence on the other end of the line. She rarely called her at work. Her immediate thought was that something had happened to Chris. That he had walked off without his cane again and wandered out into traffic. Or taken another fall, stubbornly trying to move too quickly around some unfamiliar geography.

"Everything's fine, honey," Mrs. Lawrence said when she heard Marie catch her breath. "I just wanted to let you know that somebody...some men...are in town and want to meet you. I think you will really enjoy meeting them."

"Some men? Who?"

"I'll let them introduce themselves." She paused, took a deep breath. "Chris refused to see them. He said that chapter of his life was over and he had no desire to re-visit it or anybody associated with it. I know they heard him and they traveled a long way to come see him. Marie, he embarrassed me no end. If he had been ten years younger, I would have pulled me a switch off that hedge bush out front and..."

"You know how he can be, Mom. Remember back when we actually thought his stubborn streak was cute?"

"Yes. Yes, I do. Anyway, they wanted to meet you, even after Chris turned them away. They're going to take Dad and me and you to lunch if you can go. Chris, too, but you know he won't even think about going. They say they owe all of us a lot. Everything. That's what one of them said. Everything. You'll see."

The Lawrences picked her up at the shop and headed up West End Avenue to Elliston Place Soda Shop. Before he went away, Chris and Marie stopped by often for malts and burgers when they were at the park nearby. On the ride over, neither Mr. nor Mrs. Lawrence gave her any clues about whom they were to meet for lunch. Marie had an idea, but she kept her guess to herself.

They chose a large, round table in a back corner, away from the rush and noise of the lunch crowd, and ordered sweet tea for themselves while they waited for the mysterious guests. The place was full of students from nearby Vanderbilt University, many of them clearly older than was typical, back from the recently ended war and in school. A tableful of nurses from Baptist Hospital, two blocks away, laughed and compared notes on their various patients.

Marie saw the door open and three men step inside from the street. They wore Marine dress uniforms but removed their caps immediately once inside. They squinted, trying to get their eyes accustomed to the darker interior of the restaurant after the brilliant sun outside. They slowly made their way between the tables, obviously looking for someone.

Almost immediately, as if cued by some unseen hand, the entire restaurant hushed. Every person—college student, nurse, businessman—stood and began to applaud. Even the harried waitresses stopped rushing about. Some carried trays loaded with plates and food on their shoulders. They put down their loads and clapped their hands, too. Someone cheered and then the rest of the crowd joined in.

The soldiers grinned, their faces flushed, but they waved back in appreciation, acknowledging the standing ovation.

Marie noticed at once that one of the men, a tall, slender private, had no hands, only stubs.

The one in the middle of the three, an officer, had his coat sleeve pinned to his chest. He was missing his right arm. In his good hand, he carried something familiar to the people at the back table. It was a cane used by those who had lost their sight.

The third soldier seemed whole, uninjured, except for a slight limp.

Mrs. Lawrence waved to them and got their attention amid the sudden pep rally, motioning the soldiers back to where they waited for them. The applause faded and everyone went back to his or her lunch. Still, the warmth of the greeting for these returning warriors lingered in the busy restaurant.

"Boys, this is Mr. Lawrence, Christopher's dad. And Marie. Marie Benedict. His fiancé." Mrs. Lawrence pointed to each in turn.

The first soldier shook Mr. Lawrence's hand with his the stub of an arm. The second gave him a strong but awkward upside-down shake with his left hand, the only one he had left. The third soldier, the one with the limp, simply went past Mr. Lawrence's extended hand and embraced him in a long, lingering hug.

There were no handshakes for Marie from any of them. Each soldier went straight for the long, lingering hug.

"I feel like we know all three of you already," the tall, slender soldier said as he sat in the chair across from Marie.

"We do. Chris wouldn't shut up about you all," the one-armed vet said with a grin as he found another chair and eased himself down.

"'Course we made sure he heard about our folks and our gals, too." The third soldier's face broke into a broad, handsome grin. He sat down sideways in a chair, then grabbed his right leg at the knee and moved the bottom half—the part that was clearly a prosthesis—beneath the table as he swung his body around to face them. "I'm Johnny Kovacik, from Lansing, Michigan. I appreciate the hospitality but you folks can keep this humidity down here. Otherwise, it's a nice enough place, though."

The soldier with the mangled hands cuffed his partner on the shoulder.

"Ya'll don't pay any attention to this Yankee, folks. I'm Tommy Davis from just down the road in Franklin, Tennessee."

"And I'm Lieutenant Colonel Richard Harp and you don't know anything about humidity 'til you all come visit my hometown. New Orleans, Louisiana." He pronounced it "Nawlins, Loo-zanna."

Tommy Davis was staring at Marie, grinning.

"Your picture doesn't do you justice, if you don't mind my saying so, Marie. If I may call you Marie? If old Chris ever wants to let you go..." He paused,

aware he might be on the verge of saying something that could be taken the wrong way. "Hey, we may be Tommy, Johnny, and Colonel Rich, but we have taken to calling ourselves Shadrach, Meshach and Abednego."

"That's right," Johnny said. "Chris was almost certainly our Daniel up there on that mountainside. He led us out of that fiery furnace of a foxhole, sure as Daniel did in the Bible for those guys with the funny names."

"And we owe that to him," Richard added. "To him and to you, Mr. and Mrs. Lawrence, for the way you raised him. And to you, too, Marie." He squinted in her direction. "I can see you well enough to know that you are a beautiful young lady. But you mean much more to Chris than that. I'm certain his devotion for you gave him the strength to do what he did that day. His love for you and for his God. He kept saying, 'God will show us the way. He always does. He will show us the way.' And all the time, we were bleeding and burning and the mortar shells were raining down all around us and Chris, of course, had lost his eyesight when the very first shell hit."

The waitress showed up for their order then.

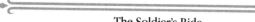

When she left, the two young soldiers and their commander began their story between swigs of the cold tea, their words spilling out as if they had held it to themselves too long already. It had to be told to the very ones who would appreciate it the most. To the ones who still did not know the details because the key player—Christopher—refused to talk about it.

The men found themselves in the same platoon when they shipped out from the States. Like many young men, away from home, headed for war and with a murky future, some spent their last nights before the battlefield looking for a good time filled with fun, drinks, fights and women while they waited until it was time to board the troopship. Most of them seemed determined to live a lifetime in a few days.

Chris Lawrence, of course, had little interest in such carryings-on. He passed his last few days in Hawaii in a different way, visiting and ministering to wounded soldiers at the hospital. He even talked a chaplain into letting him bring the message at a church service near the base.

"Chris was almost too good to be true," Richard said. "I was a major then—a lieutenant colonel

now—I have prepared and led plenty of young men into battle. I figured there had to be something wrong with Chris. Nobody could be that good. I know now that was probably just envy. We all only wished we could be as fine a man as Christopher Lawrence."

All three soldiers nodded.

Johnny Kovacik was born Catholic but had drifted far away from church in his teen years.

Richard Harp, too, but he had never been much of a churchgoer anyhow. He grew up in the streets of the French Quarter, surrounded by drugs, whiskey, and prostitutes. He hoped the priest did not see him doing the things he did before he could get into the confessional and make it right.

Tommy Davis was a self-proclaimed Baptist backslider and could not understand why anyone would rather visit the sick and read the Bible with injured soldiers instead of going out and getting roaring drunk while trying to pick up anything in a skirt.

"We may not live to see this place again," Tommy told Chris. "God won't mind a bit if we kick up our heels and blow off a little steam. He'll understand."

"That's exactly why we need to do the right thing

because we may not make it out of this thing in one piece," Chris countered seriously, just before breaking into a good-natured grin. "Besides, if we ever end up flat on our backs like those poor fellows, I hope somebody will come read the Bible and pray with us."

The younger soldiers laughed and made fun of Chris, renamed him 'Preacher,' and continued to go out each night, looking for something that made them feel alive, invincible. They usually found trouble. Or it found them.

Richard Harp would simply shake his head and go on with his duty, getting things ready to ship out. He was glad to have somebody like Christopher Lawrence. That was simply one less soldier he would have to worry about retrieving from the brig or sick bay.

On their final night in Hawaii, though, Chris did not go to the hospital or attend a prayer vigil at the chapel. Instead, he stayed in the barracks to write letters to Marie and his parents. And at 10 o'clock, two hours before they were due back from leave, Tommy and Johnny showed up at the barracks, well ahead of the time Major Harp usually made his final rounds to make sure everyone had made it back in one piece. Tommy and Johnny had been drinking but they were hardly drunk.

"Preacher, you sure know how to spoil a soldier's last night of leave," Tommy told Chris. "Shaming us into coming back here early and writing letters home when we could be getting into some serious mischief."

But they were thanking him the next morning when they were roused early to form up in lines and march down to their next ride, the big troop ship that would carry them to an island in the South Pacific.

Chris took advantage of the ride across the Pacific Ocean to talk with each of his best friends. By the time their troop ship was within sight of the beach on Iwo Jima, all four of the men took time to pray together, the officer right there on his knees next to the three enlisted men. They all read their military-issued Bibles and asked Chris basic questions about what the scriptures meant. They had found a better way to feel alive, invincible.

The troops landed on the black-sand beach the next morning. Chris and his platoon waded ashore and climbed to the top of the beach. They were met by stillness—no enemy fire at all. According to the voices on the radio, the enemy had retreated into the mountains that made up the other half of the small island. The smoke and damage along the beach resulted from the bombing and strafing of friendly aircraft, softening up the landing zone for them, not from enemy cannons.

As they pushed into the thick jungle, the chatter of machinegun fire, the yelps from those bitten by the bullets, and the thud of distant artillery hidden in the mountains confirmed what they suspected. The enemy had waited for them to come into range. The peaceful landing quickly became war. Artillery shells fell all around them, grinding into their ranks, but the ships sitting offshore and the aircraft that buzzed overhead had a hard time spotting the guns. They hid in valleys or in caves along the mountain-side, camouflaged perfectly. They spat out their huge shells and pulled back into the caves and crevices, the openings covered with camouflaged curtains.

The Japanese troops came out primarily at night in vicious hunting parties, surprising Marines in their foxholes or tents, ripping them with gunfire and then in hand-to-hand combat before retreating at sunrise into the honeycomb caverns, out of reach.

That night Chris, Tommy, and Johnny were part of a squad sent to dig in on a small plateau, almost directly beneath a series of caves that pocked the side of the island's highest mountain. Major Richard Harp led the patrol. This particular mission was that important.

They knew a huge enemy artillery piece was hidden away in a cave several hundred feet above them. Their job was to watch for the Japanese to roll the massive gun to the cave entrance to ready it for firing at American positions arrayed along the beach far below. Then, the Marines were to call in artillery shots and aircraft to blast the enemy gun and its hiding place into pieces. The Marines needed to dig in, mostly in darkness, and remain undetected by the frequent passing patrols during the night. First light usually brought the barrage and they would be in perfect position to direct the attack by radio.

Once the coordinates were reported, but before the shooting began, Chris and his buddies would have to scurry down the mountainside or risk catching the brunt of the attack from their own people. The friendly fire would almost certainly be fatal considering their strategic location.

They dug in as best they could in the hard, rocky volcanic soil. They tried to stay out of sight amid the scrubby bushes that grew there. There was no light to read their Bibles that night, so they simply talked. Talked quietly about how much their outlook on religion, Jesus, and salvation had been transformed in the last few months. Each man acknowledged that it was Chris Lawrence who had prompted the about-face in their lives.

Something about the man, the intensity of his blue eyes, and the way he had of making it all so simple when he explained even the most esoteric points grabbed them. He had already told them of his plans to be a minister. No one was surprised. They had no doubts he would be a truly great shepherd, an effective fisher of men.

That night, Chris quoted from memory Deuteronomy 20. "When you go to war against your enemies and see horses and chariots and an army greater than yours, do not be afraid of them, because the Lord your God will be with you."

As all the men in the foxhole listened to Chris's soft recitation, they gazed at the tiny pinpoints of light that were American ships lying at sea, out of reach of the enemy guns but close enough so their own immense shells could reach most of the island, including the cave above them. It was hard to tell where the light-studded sea and horizon ended and the star-filled sky began. It was moonless and, thankfully, very dark. They could hear the distant sound of machine gun fire, the occasional shout of someone hit, the thunder of distant grenade explosions. A time or two, they even heard the voices of enemy patrols passing nearby and below them, unaware any Marines had managed to penetrate this far.

Chris preached quietly, making sure his words did not drift up to the cave entrance above them or that they might be overheard by the patrols below.

"Each person's life is a journey along a mostly unfamiliar stretch of road," he said. "As we take life's ride, we never know what lies around the next curve or over the next hill. It could be something wonderful, a triumph for a loved one, a tragedy for another. A victory. A loss. The road has twists and turns. Sometimes our progress seems too slow. There are bumps and rough road. But with the help of our faith, our family, our friends, we have the ability to continue our ride toward the ultimate reward at the end of the journey."

As the men ate their lunches with Chris's family that day in the diner, each of the three soldiers recounted how meaningful the words had been, especially on that particular dark, star-filled night. They knew their mission the next day would be dangerous, that they might well encounter the enemy as they abandoned their post on the mountainside. However, knowing something better awaited them at the end of their journey comforted them whether it was many, many miles past the next bump in the road or that their journey might end violently before the next nightfall.

"That right there would have been enough," Richard Harp testified as he chewed the last of his cheeseburger. "Just giving us the benefit of his faith and convincing us that we had a reward at the end of the road. That was something special for all of us in that foxhole that night. I have to think it was special for Chris, too. His whispered words were simply too powerful. He had Divine help crafting them."

They awoke well before daylight the next morning, eating their K-rations, when suddenly the ground seemed to tremble beneath them. They could see the barrel of the big artillery piece in the dim twilight, just protruding from the burlap curtain that hid the cave from the troops below, the aircraft, the Allied ships.

Chris first fired up the radio from within the foxhole but could not get anyone to answer his call. He decided he needed to move to increase his chances of being heard. He crawled on his stomach to the edge of the bluff, dragging his radio behind him, to hide beneath a scraggly bush, as much out of sight as he could get. He was in danger of the enemy seeing him, though. Still, he knew that this location would give him a better signal and the best angle to direct incoming fire to the artillery piece.

Lying on his belly in the dirt, he whispered into the microphone trying to raise his contact on the radio and report the numbers that would allow the ship's guns to train in on the enemy weapon. The other soldiers, at Major Harp's direction, spread out in a circle inside the rough foxhole, each facing in a different direction, looking for any patrolling enemy who might stumble upon them before they could report the precise spot where the big gun poked through the burlap at the mouth of the cave.

They would never know for certain what went wrong. Probably, though, it was someone else below, or out there on the deck of one of the ships, who spotted the gun barrel first—maybe a glint of light reflected from the first rays of the rising sun. They reported it to someone else who immediately gave the command to begin firing—someone who did not know of the presence of Chris and his fellow soldiers who were dug in on the ledge just below the target.

Just as Chris put the microphone to his lips to attempt to give the coordinates, a deadly hailstorm of shells suddenly began to land all around them. American shells, homing in on the big gun.

One of those shells landed in the middle of the circle of Marines. Another erupted right in front of Chris. The concussion of that explosion, like an unseen hand, violently flipped him up into the air and over onto his back. He lay there for a moment, wondering if he was alive or dead. His vision was gone and he was almost deaf. He could see noth-

ing, not the morning sky, not the dust and smoke of the exploding ordnance that continued to fall from the sky, seemingly without end. Nor could he hear anything but a muffled roar, distant shouts, as if he were deep under water.

He could still feel the wind from the blasts, the heat and concussion of their explosions peppering his skin with dirt and gravel. He must still be alive. He touched his face and it was slick with blood, but he felt little pain.

Through the roar in his ears, he could hear the cries of his buddies a bit more clearly, enough to know they were in trouble. He had already deduced that the ordnance that was tearing them apart was friendly, from American guns. He had to find a way to make it stop.

Somehow, he managed to locate the radio in the blackness. He felt its case and it seemed to be in one piece. He held onto the strap and began to crawl back to where the foxhole should have been. It took him an eternity to get there.

Johnny lay on his side, unable to move, and watched Chris inch toward him. Johnny's legs seemed to be broken but he really could not tell if they were both still there. He was having trouble moving the right one and when he flexed the other one, horrible pain shot up the length of his body.

"Go the other way, Chris!" Johnny shouted to him, not caring if the enemy heard him. Chris was crawling over open ground. Any enemy soldier nearby would see him if the shelling stopped. Of course, one of those shells could land right on top of him, too. Johnny knew his friend needed to run in the other direction, away from the target zone. And he needed to do it as fast as he could go, and then drop off the ledge behind him and, if the fall did not kill him, he could crawl out of the fire zone and attempt to save himself. "Don't worry about us! Go the other way!"

Johnny could see that blood covered Chris's face, his eyes squinted shut. It was clear that Chris could not see where he was going, and he was now closer to the foxhole than he was to the ledge.

"Okay, come this way. Crawl this way. They'll move off the top of us in a minute, surely."

Another couple of nearby explosions cut off his words. Johnny raised his head and looked for the others. Several members of the patrol were in bits,

gone. Richard Harp, their commander, lay half out of the foxhole but was now sliding back in, his uniform covered with blood on the right side and his face twisted in pain. Tommy was thirty feet away, leaning against the rock wall of the mountain, apparently where one of the explosions hurled his body. His face was white and he held his hands at his chest. They were bleeding badly.

"Where are you, Johnny? Say something," Chris shouted at him, spitting blood and dirt from his mouth.

"Right here, Preacher. Right here. Another ten feet and you'll slide right in next to me."

Another shell exploded between them and Johnny ducked. When he looked at Chris again, he fully expected to see him in pieces, but he was still crawling, dragging the radio. Somehow, he made it and ended up next to his buddy.

"How are you, Johnny?"

"Fine as I can be. Some of the others need help. Tommy's losing a lot of blood. So is the Major. We got to get somebody up here."

"First we have to get this shelling stopped or..."

Another blast erupted right where Chris had

been only seconds before, covering them with dirt and chunks of rocks.

Chris felt his way and set the radio back on top of the edge of the hole, exposed again to anyone who might look down from above. He and his radio would be an easy target.

"You'll have to help me, Johnny. Tell me what the frequency dial says. It has F-R-E-Q below it. Say it loud. I'm deaf and blind."

Kovacik pulled himself up as much as he could, ignoring the intense pain that ran the length of his legs.

"Looks like 3.2."

"I'm going to turn the knob. Let me know when it's on 2.5. Okay?"

Squinting through the sweat in his own eyes, Johnny could hardly see the dial, but when it looked like it read the correct radio channel, he told Chris to stop. Chris pulled the radio's headset to a bloody ear and pushed the button on its side.

"Red Fox, Red Fox, this is Tango Six, Tango Six. Read me?"

He tried repeatedly but only heard a humming in his ear. Then he realized the audio gain control was too low for him to hear above the roar in his head. He handed the headset to Johnny and told him what to say. Somehow, the two of them working together were able to make contact and convince someone that the shelling had to stop, that there were wounded men up there on that mountainside who needed help—American soldiers who were taking the brunt of the attack, not the Japanese artillery piece.

A team soon found them, based on the information Chris provided. They quickly gathered up the wounded and headed back down the hill before the enemy could stick their heads out of the cave and spot them.

They would later determine that Chris crawled blindly over open ground in the middle of the artillery attack for over 100 feet. If he had gone the other way, and even if he had survived the fall down the ledge, the radio's weak signal would likely not have been able to reach the forward post. As he suspected, he would not have been able to stop the shelling and summon help from any less elevation. Another man—a lesser man—might have gone that way, trying to save himself, leaving his platoon behind to die.

Had he not done what he did that morning, the three survivors in the foxhole would have certainly bled to death.

Colonel Harp took a long drink and drained his glass of sweet tea. He looked hard at the table, found an empty spot, and set the glass down carefully.

"That is delicious stuff!" he said, and smacked his lips. "But you know, it seems like everything tastes sweeter now than it used to, before I met your boy. Your fiancé. He changed my life for the better, folks, and I mean before we ever got to that mountain."

Several of them had ordered malted milks and were slurping up the last of it. Mr. Lawrence was taking the final bite of his apple pie. The restaurant lunch crowd had cleared out considerably. They were the only ones left. Nobody hurried them.

"We owe him so much," Johnny said. "The first payment is due right now."

"So that's our story, folks," Tommy told them. "Now, you tell us what we need to do to help get the preacher back on the road."

The Intervention

It took quite a bit of selling on her part, but Marie finally coerced Chris to take a ride with her that afternoon. It was a beautiful spring day, begging to be experienced. He needed to get out of the house. She had taken the afternoon off and she told him how much she would appreciate his company on a short drive around town. His mother fixed a picnic snack for them, fried peach pies and a jug of sweet iced tea.

"Do whatever you want to do. You don't need to drag me around," he told Marie, his voice toneless, almost as if he was tired of fighting her and his parents. "No point in me going sightseeing, I don't think."

"You need to get out and get some fresh air, Chris," she said, taking his arm and guiding him toward the front door. He pulled away from her when they neared the car—still his ride, the car he and his dad restored together—and made a point of locating the passenger-side door handle all by himself, opening the door and sitting down.

"Yeah, it is a beautiful day," he said, his voice heavy with sarcasm. "Look at those flowers. Those clouds. Oh, I think that one looks like a horse. And there's a bat. A blind bat."

She ignored him as she cranked the car. It still ran smoothly, just like the day he drove it away on his first venture away from home. And he was correct about one thing. It was a beautiful late-spring day, with flowers lining front porches all along the street. She liked to think he smelled them. That was how he knew to mock her with their mention.

"Your car running to suit you?" she asked him.

"Yeah, maybe I'll try to get around to giving her a tune-up. When I finish painting the house and reading the encyclopedia. Shouldn't take long. I could even do it in the dark. Daylight. Night. Makes no difference to me." He glanced over at her. "See, I am trying to find the good in all this, just like you and my folks keep griping at me to do."

She bit her lip, telling herself his bitterness was not actually aimed at her at all. No, he gave equal doses to her, his mother, his father, the preacher,

the folks from the veterans' hospital who stopped by to help him learn Braille and teach him how to navigate in his still-new, dark world. She had almost gotten used to his sarcasm, but there was no denying that it still hurt her sometimes.

Maybe this ride would be the first step to bringing him back.

"I heard that some of your Marine buddies came by to see you this morning," she finally said. "You know you really should have seen them." Then, as she always did when she made some mention of "seeing" or "looking," she bit her lip and corrected herself. "Sorry, 'visited' with them."

"For what? I know they have their own problems. What would we do, sit around and compare stitches and amputations?"

"They just wanted to say 'thank you.' They really do love you, Chris, and they appreciate what you did for them."

"I did not do anything. Called in a message, gave a few coordinates. I wish people would quit making it sound like I won the war singlehandedly. I was a soldier. I did my duty. But I still left pieces of my platoon on that island. I failed them. End of story."

"That's not what they think. They have a whole different perspective from yours on what happened." She made the turn onto West End Avenue, toward Centennial Park. "It's what you did before that, too. You did as much for their souls as you did for their lives. Everything that happened was part of God's plan. Every bump in the road, every single twist and turn is God's plan, Chris."

He was quiet for a while, his face turned toward the open car window. The warm breeze blew his carefully parted hair out of place but he made no move to straighten it. He needed a haircut, she thought. But he was still so handsome, even with the tiny scars below the dark glasses he always wore.

Marie had prayed at length about what she was about to do. She felt led to go ahead with it, even though she had no idea if it would crack the rock-like shell Chris Lawrence had built around himself. There was always the chance it would only drive him deeper into his self-made insulation, make it more difficult to reach him with logic or prayer.

Chris did not speak again until she turned off West End Avenue onto the street that wound in front of the Parthenon. She steered the car toward the

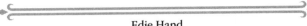
duck pond near the park's band shell, to the spot where they spent so much time before he left for the war, talking, planning, kissing, praying about their future together.

"I know where we are. I know where you are going. I even have an idea what you are doing."

"We opened up our hearts to each other plenty of times here," she said. "Maybe we can do that again, Chris."

He did not respond.

She parked, slid out, and walked around to open his door. Then, as she usually did, she allowed him get out of the car on his own. He did not resist as she led him to a park bench and sat him down. The ground was uneven and roots from the huge elms made the footing a bit difficult. That was one reason she chose this place. He would not be able to stand and run without stumbling or encountering a tree or water.

They sat there together on the bench for several minutes. Neither spoke. Ducks squawked in the distance as they jockeyed for June bugs, songbirds serenaded them from the choir loft of elm limbs above, and the gentle breeze bore the perfume from a bank

of beautiful roses—already in colorful bloom—that rimmed a part of the lake nearby.

She wished he could see the brilliant reflection of the roses in the water, that he could watch the first tendrils of color spread across the sky as the sun sank beyond the far end of the park. She knew he smelled the flowers. She knew he always enjoyed the breeze on his face and the birds' songs that accompanied their talks.

Chris did not acknowledge any of that this particular afternoon. He sat there, his head slightly tilted, as if he was trying to shut off all his senses before he accidentally enjoyed something again.

That or prepare his parry to her verbal jousting.

Suddenly it became clear that he had not shut off his senses at all. On the contrary, he had them on full receive.

"Who else is here?" he abruptly but calmly asked her. "I hear someone breathing over there." He pointed to his left. Colonel Richard Harp sat on the end of a park bench pulled close to face where Chris and Marie sat. "And I know that cologne. John Kovacik used it when he went out carousing in Hawaii before we were deployed." He pointed upwind, to where Kovacik sat on the other end of Harp's bench, what was left of his bad leg stretched out on the seat. "Unless I miss my guess, there is one other member of this little ambush party and he is most likely over there somewhere."

"Looks like the blind guy still has some of his senses left," Tommy Davis said from a few feet in front of them. He was seated in the fragrant grass between the two benches. "Not sense, mind you. I don't think he has much of that left. Senses."

"So you guys came back to poke fun at the cripple, huh?"

"Something like that," Harp said. "You sure seem to be a bundle of good times these days and no way we were going to miss out on that. No, we just want to tell you a few things that you have needed to hear for a long, long time now. You may as well sit there next to the woman who loves you and listen to us. It won't hurt you and, God knows, it might do you some good."

"Like I could jump up and run if I wanted to. My driver license expired, too, you know. Guess I forgot to renew it."

"I'd have a tough time running, too," Kovacik

retorted. "Running is no longer an option. If you had not been so wrapped up in self-pity, you might have gotten around to checking on those of us whose lives you managed to save that day. Each of us has had his own cross to bear since then. See, I planned to go back to school when I got out of the Marines. I was a pretty good football player in high school, if I do say so myself. We won the Michigan state championship my senior year. Several colleges had talked to me before I enlisted. I lost a leg on that island. It may be buried out there in that black dirt, but it still itches like crazy sometimes. No matter how hard I scratch this wooden leg, it won't stop itching.

"See, Preacher, that little episode changed my plans just a little bit, too, you know. I stewed about it for a while. I shook my fist at God and told him what I thought of this little bump in the road he laid out for me. But the more I thought about it, the more I remembered some things you told us, Preacher. The parable of the talents. I don't remember where it is in the Bible…"

"Matthew," Chris said. "'Well done my good and faithful servant.'"

"Okay. Matthew. I'm getting there, but I got a late

start. But you know what? I am going back to school. I want to coach, probably football and basketball. But there is more. I plan on having a positive influence on young men and women, just the way you did on old Shadrach, Meshach and Abednego here. You gave me that idea, Preacher. You and a coach or two that kept me out of trouble back when I played ball."

Kovacik watched Chris's face in the twilight, hoping to see some sign that he was listening, that he was understanding what Johnny was telling him, how important these changes were to his life after the war.

There was no such indication.

"I played the piano, you know," Tommy Davis said. "Played in church, in honky-tonks, anywhere I found one, ever since I was six or seven years old. I never had a lesson but before I joined the Marines, I already had written several cheatin' and drinkin' country and western songs that were recorded by artists whose names you would know. Some here in Nashville. I had been jotting down some more cheatin' and drinkin' songs in a notebook and was going to finish them when I got back from the war.

"Chris, when you showed me the light, it got me to thinking about my road ahead. I immediately began hearing melodies and started writing songs in my head, thinking about all the good I could do through my music. I tore those other songs out of that notebook and threw them away. When we were on that island, I started filling up pages with lyrics. It was like God was dictating them to me. I couldn't wait to get to a piano and start adding the melodies."

Davis looked at where his hands had once been, then at Chris, sitting there impassively on the park bench.

"It's impossible to play a piano without fingers and hands," Davis resumed. "Mine got blown away that day right at the wrists. But after I did a bit of my own soul-searching, asking a lot of questions and getting no answer from God, I finally realized that He had answered those questions long before. Back when I sang 'Power in the Blood' and played those other great old hymns on that old out-of-tune piano at Beulah Baptist. You had more answers for me when you talked about life's road, how we can get ourselves knocked into the ditch, but we emerge stronger if we climb out and get back on the high-way. Remember? That night on the island before our own guys blew heck out of us? The church we had in that foxhole that night?"

He tried to see some sign on Chris's face that he was feeling what he was telling him. There was still no reaction, no indication he was hearing a word his friends were saying.

"I have already renewed my connections to people in the music business here in Nashville. I was going to show them the songs as soon as I got back. About the only musical instrument I can play with these hands now is a conga drum. But I can get somebody to transcribe the notes and words and pick them out on my piano. And I can sing them well enough to do demos. I've got five placed already and they keep coming. Looks like the Lord wants me to write about a million of them. But I don't care. I'll write a billion if He asks me to, if that is the best thing I can do to lead somebody else through his own rough patch of road. One's called 'A Miracle in Me,' about having faith even if you are not sure what kind of ride you have ahead of you. 'I walk in faith and trust in things I can't even see 'cause I believe there's a miracle in me.' I love that line, even if I did write it! There's another one called 'The Soldier's Ride' about how a young soldier leaves on a troop train not knowing what kind of ride will eventually bring him home again—a train, a plane, a wheelchair, a hearse.

"I'm working on the melody for one now about the ones left behind when we go marching off to do our duty. 'Learning to Say Goodbye.' It's about telling a soldier goodbye when he leaves home. About soldiers saying goodbye to their own when they leave them on a battlefield. The words came easy. They poured out of my heart. Chris, I don't care if only one or two people hear those songs if they make a difference to them."

Richard Harp chuckled.

"Well, Chris, my football days were over before they started, and when I sing, pelicans scatter and small children run to their mothers in fright. God blessed me with a different talent. You never knew I could cook, did you? We only had the K-rations or the mess hall food during training and when we shipped, and then when we were out there fighting. Man, did I miss the jambalaya and gumbo and the grilled seafood with the Cajun spices I always made special. Cook that fish over some mesquite wood, throw some of those mysterious, magic spices on them. Man! You know, there is something about New Orleans. Maybe it's the humidity or the river or the heat over the bayous that simmers up such a special stewpot. Probably has something to do with it being such a melting pot of people from different cultures.

"See, if you grow up there, you either absorb music until you play it real good—and, as I said, I couldn't carry a tune in a bucket with a lid—or you pick up cooking by osmosis. I was going to come back from the war to the 'Big Easy' and open a restaurant. I even had me a spot picked out right there in the Garden District that would be perfect. I had plans for making and distributing my Creole seafood dip, too. Then that artillery shell blew up in my face, took my arm, made a mess of my eyes. Shoot, who could ever imagine a one-armed cook who is legally blind—I can see a dozen eggs or a sack of flour well enough to make out what they are, but I could never read a recipe or see the ingredients on the label of a can of something through this peephole God left me—well, what kind of chef is that? The whole idea of becoming the 'Cookin' Colonel' seemed to have died."

Colonel Harp leaned closer to try to see if he might be finally getting any response, but shadows now covered Chris's face.

"I lay there in that bed at the hospital, listening to the sounds of those other boys all around me, all in such pain. In my dreams, I kept seeing the faces of the others who died there on that mountain that morning, wondering what I could have done to prevent it. I admit I got depressed about my situation, too. Who wouldn't? Then, just like Tommy, I got to thinking about something you said when we held church in that foxhole the night before...well, before we all got hurt. When you talked about life's journey, you mentioned when Jesus was choosing his disciples, he made it clear that they were not being chosen to serve a king. Their job was to help Him help those who were hurting. Jesus sent word to John that, through Him, the blind receive their sight, and the lame walk, the lepers are cleansed, and the deaf hear, the dead are raised up, and the poor have the gospel preached to them. That was what He was all about. I can't begin to tell you how much those words meant to me in that sickbed with all that death and pain swirling around me."

Harp paused to get his breath. Chris cleared his throat.

"That's Matthew again," he said in a quiet voice. "Matthew chapter eleven."

"Yes. Yes it is. And even now, it still means so much to me. I made the decision to climb right back up onto the roadway and keep traveling toward where I wanted to be. Where the Lord wanted me to be. As soon as I got back home, I started transcribing my Creole cookbook. I got to where I was pretty good on the typewriter even with one hand and seeing a letter or two at a time if I put my nose right down to the paper. I finished it by myself, testing every recipe on family members, the local firemen in the station on Poydras Street, anybody who would agree to sample whatever I created. I got to be pretty popular and I don't think I killed anybody with my recipes.

"Preacher, my cookbook is going to be published. I just signed a contract. I have partners—each of them war veterans, a couple of them with a nick or two to show for their trouble—and we're talking about opening the restaurant, The Cooking Colonel's Creole Cuisine, in the Garden District. I'm talking with some people about putting my seafood dip on the market in New Orleans. We already have distributors interested in taking it nationwide. People are seeing a lot of the world during the war and they will be more receptive to different kinds of food now than they have ever been. That's my good luck. My good luck and God's will at work."

Chris finally showed some reaction to the words of his friends, shaking his head, a wry smile on his face. He lifted his hand from his lap and pointed at each of the other men.

"Okay, you all three had hopes and dreams. You lost them. Now you're getting them back. That has nothing to do with me or my situation. I'm happy for you guys. I really am. But you know that any one of you would have called in that radio report that day and everything would have worked out, just the same. If I had made the radio call a few minutes quicker, the friendly fire would never have happened. None of you would have been hurt. Those other guys up there on that ledge would still be alive. I should have saved them, fellows. God should have helped me save them. It's that simple. I didn't save them from dying. I didn't save you three from being hurt." Chris choked back tears. "I don't know if God failed me or I failed God. Maybe both. Maybe this was God's way of slapping me down, punishing me for not doing all I could do that day. I was the one who was going to preach and I'll never be able to do that. You can coach, write songs, publish cookbooks all you want to. Maybe you are just much better people than I am. You guys did that on your own. The only thing that God is telling me to do is sit back, shut up, and make brooms the rest of my life."

Chris paused and dropped his hands back into his lap. The gesture was one of utter and complete hopelessness.

"Preacher, we came here today for two reasons." Tommy Davis spoke quietly, leaning forward.

"That's right," Johnny Kovacik chimed in. "First , we wanted to tell you face to face how much we appreciate what you did. No medal or commendation can do that. We knew we had to do it in person, and we came here to do just that. Much as you diminish it, you crawled across a hundred feet of hell on that ledge with bombs crashing down all around you. It was a miracle that you managed to make it to that foxhole at all. It was another miracle that you got the radio working and talked me through finding the right channel and getting the shelling stopped. That we were able to get help so quickly. That a friendly patrol was nearby and we didn't all four bleed to death waiting for somebody who just happened to have enough plasma to keep us alive. That all happened with God's help. Maybe you are not hearing what God is telling you. Maybe your soul is as blind as your eyes. It's the same thing He told each of us. We—me, Tommy, Colonel Harp, and you—we survived that day on that island because He had a plan for us. By the way, did you know that they shelled that big artillery piece hard after they hauled us out of the way that morning. They put her right out of commission. No telling how many soldiers are alive and with their families today because of what we did to help take out that gun. Four days later, they raised the American flag on top of that mountain. The battle for the island was not over yet, but it had turned. You have to take some pride in that."

"See, Chris, that is the first thing we came to tell you," Harp joined in. "That everything has a purpose in God's plan. We accomplished our mission that day. We helped in our own way. Win enough little skirmishes on mountainsides and you win the battle. Win enough battles, you win the war. That is what soldiers do. That is what we did. But there's more."

"Yes, I'm going to coach sports," Johnny added, "but my minor in school is Religion and I am going to be a witness to everyone I come in contact with. Whether I win games or not, I'll do my duty to my God. I made him plenty promises I intend to keep."

"I am writing songs that will glorify God and I hope to reach millions with their message," Tommy said. "If I do, I'll make money, win awards, get glorified, but that is nothing compared to what I will get at the end of life's road."

Harp added, "My cookbook has recipes for Creole seafood dip and Cajun cornbread and gumbo but it also has a chapter urging those who try the recipes to say grace with a humble heart, thanking God for what he has provided. I also have suggestions on how to increase the recipes at little cost so there will be enough to share with someone else who has no food. There will be a line of scripture on every bottle

of spice we sell. I hope those simple verses will uplift somebody at a time when they most need it."

"Okay, okay. You all caught religion. But what was the second thing you said that you wanted to tell me?" Chris asked.

Marie's eyes grew large and she took his hand in hers. It was the first sign of interest in anything from him that she had seen since he came back home. She tried not to hope it was the breakthrough she had prayed for, but she silently prayed anyway.

All three soldiers stood and came to stand next to their comrade, helping each other over the rough ground. Each put a hand on his shoulder. Chris did not flinch but only kept his face straight ahead, toward where the darkness was falling across the lake and the ducks had retreated to shore. The dark mirror-like water was already reflecting the first star of the evening. Chris could not see it, of course, and the others were not looking.

"Chris, you absolutely saved our lives that morning on Iwo Jima," Harp said.

"You saved our lives so we could go out and help others," Johnny added. "But the real saving started months before in the barracks, before we ever

shipped out, and, thank God, it continued that night in the foxhole."

"Right, Preacher," Tommy said, tightening his grip on Chris's shoulder. "You prolonged our lives by, maybe, fifty years with your bravery and determination that day. But you gave us the opportunity to live for eternity with what you taught us before then—us and several other of the boys who did not make it that day. See, Chris. You did save those boys, no matter what you say."

Marie squeezed Chris's hand even harder and placed her head on his shoulder.

"I admit that I was mad at God, too, darling," she said, her eyes filling with tears. Nevertheless, her voice was strong and her words clear. She had rehearsed them for a long, long time. "Mad at Him for taking you away to war before we could even begin our lives together exactly the way we planned. I was madder still when He brought you back from the war wounded and lost. But then I realized that His plan was still working. Certainly not the way you and I pictured and schemed for it to work. But there was a reason you lost your sight out there. A reason why you have had to go through this time of soul-

searching and questioning. Your friends here—the men whose lives and souls you helped save—found their part in the plan already, Chris. Through your witnessing and your bravery, you have given them the chance to spread the word and help others and they are already such strong vessels. That is what soldiers do. They fight battles so the right things are set into motion. So people are free. So evil is over-come. You did your duty. You bravely accomplished you mission. You made sure these men can now do their next duty."

She kissed him on his cheek.

"Now they have come to witness the way you showed them. They came to show you that you will get another chance, too, Christopher Wren Lawrence. You cannot change what has happened but you have another chance to make a difference in people's lives. Another chance to save people the way you so bravely did that morning with that radio and the last bit of strength you had. When you do, only God knows how many people will be set free, how many other lives will be saved for eternity because you have taken your talents and your strength and put them to use for that purpose. That is when you will finally overcome this patch of rough road, realize you have been made stronger by it, and continue on the ride God has laid out for you. That is when you will finally be free of all this pain and once again have hope."

She was quiet then, holding his hand in both of hers. She let go, reached into her pocket and slid a small, smooth courage stone into his palm.

"Have faith in things you cannot see. Have hope that faith will prevail. Let this stone serve as a reminder that you are never alone, that you are surrounded by those who love you and by the love of your Lord."

The three other men still touched him, each praying silently as Marie spoke.

It was almost too dark to see it, but Marie did not miss it.

A single tear rolled down Christopher Lawrence's cheek and dropped where their hands intertwined.

A baptism, she thought. A baptism.

The Third Angel

Diana Meade suddenly jumped off the bench and ran the few steps it took for her to reach the grave and marker where Christopher W. Lawrence rested. She kneeled there and touched the name engraved on the stone, tracing the single initial in the middle with her fingertips.

"I knew it! The 'W' is for 'Wren!' Wren Lawrence! The evangelist. The famous evangelist!" She clapped her hands like the cheerleader she once was, as if her team just scored the winning touchdown. She stood and turned back to where the old storyteller sat, a whimsical grin on his face as he watched her joy upon realizing that the pieces of her dream fit together. "I did not know he was buried here, in this cemetery. Even in Nashville. I figured he would have been in Arlington National or a private spot some- where with a huge memorial befitting such a rich and powerful man."

"He would not have had it any other way," the

old man said. "He told Marie he wanted his earthly remains to be buried here when he passed. Here among his fellow soldiers, like a young man they are going to bury over yonder directly. She agreed. He didn't make a big deal of it and few people know about it. He preached all along that the grave is not your final resting spot. Maybe for the body, but not for the soul. He didn't want the buses running through here either, just to show off his grave and cross to tourists."

Diana came back and sat next to Claude again. She still thought it a bit odd that these two old people who claimed to be angels—Celia and Claude—knew so much of the story behind the man buried beneath the nearby cross. Odd that they were willing to spend so much time telling her about him, too.

"I knew Wren Lawrence," Diana told Claude. "I did some charity work with him, with a foundation my husband and I were getting started for sick kids. We had big plans for the foundation but we needed someone powerful and charismatic to help us. He was truly a great man, selfless, inspirational. Even though he was a world-famous preacher, he clearly felt closest to the common man, to children, to those

who were hurting. That's why I wanted his help with that project of ours. I knew he was a war hero but I didn't know the whole story. I appreciate you—you and Celia—telling me all this."

The old man smiled and nodded. Still ignoring the sandwich on the bench between him and her, he went on.

"There's more. You see, that was part of the deal he made with Marie, Tommy, Colonel Harp and Johnny. When he finally realized that God was not finished with him, he decided to re-start his drive to the ministry, he made it clear that it would absolutely not be based on his war history. He wanted to minister to war vets, soldiers, and their families, but he wanted to do it on his own terms, not based on his being a disabled veteran with a medal for courage the size of a wagon wheel. He did not want to flaunt his heroism. He was just another soldier who went to war for his country and did his duty. He wanted to talk to military men and women on that level."

Diana was only half listening to the old man by then. Something was nagging at her.

"I never heard him use his first name—Christopher," Diana said.

"His folks named him after Christopher Wren, that British feller that built so many churches. They hoped that their first-born son would one day build churches, too. He wasn't interested in the brick or stone kind, though. He wanted to build the kind where it was church anytime two or more gathered in His name. That's why he dropped the 'Christopher' part. He did what he set out to do, too. You notice he did a lot of his preaching in hospitals, schools, prisons. His television show was always filmed in some simple place: foundries, warehouses, barns, cornfields, and he was surrounded by real people. He did not like to preach in some big, spectacular church building like some. And his prediction about something coming along even more powerful than radio? His television shows are still running. He reached millions, right there in their dens and living rooms. In hotel rooms. Bars. He swore in two presidents, you know. And he preached the funeral for the 'Cookin' Colonel.' But his favorite service took place when he just sat down and talked with a platoon of soldiers on a drill field or a bunch of steelworkers within sight of the blast furnaces. No stained glass. No rows of pews. No choir. Just him and the people."

Diana Meade leaned back and shut her eyes, her head spinning. Her feet were still shoeless and she wriggled her toes in the cool grass, not even worrying anymore about her hose.

What an amazing story! Wren Lawrence had probably been the most recognized religious figure in the country until his death a few years before. Unlike others, there was never a hint of scandal or hypocrisy. He insisted on a simple existence, a modest home. His wife, Marie, remained in the background. So much so that Diana had not made the connection until she realized who "Christopher" really was. Now, thanks to Celia and Claude and the mystical tale they were spinning, she knew the winding road Wren Lawrence had traveled to get to where he did, to be able to wield the positive influence he did over others. She only appreciated him more.

Now she knew. Chris and Marie did continue their journey together after all. They had four children. Two, she remembered, were continuing his ministry. The other two were physicians who established hospitals in impoverished regions of the world.

The intervention in the park with the men whose lives he saved did exactly what it set out to do. It put

Chris back on the path. But as much as Diana read and heard about the renowned evangelist, she had never heard that part of his story.

"We had big plans for our foundation," Diana finally said with a sigh, her eyes still closed as a breeze swept over her. A summer rain was marching her way. She could feel it. She did not care. "Dr. Lawrence was going to help us get things set up. Lord knows we had enough money and contacts in the music industry to raise enough cash to do some good for the children's' hospitals. But I got busy with my job. I guess I got intoxicated by the power that money brings and I lost sight of my dream. I ended up settling for something that fed my ego and my bank account but not my soul. Jeff's unit was called up for the first Gulf War and he spent six months in Kuwait. Then it was like we were strangers after he came home, him getting his practice back in order, me trying to make all the money there was. Our marriage went bad just as our careers were occupying so much of our time. Robbie was healthy again, in remission. I guess we just let the idea slide. Dr. Lawrence called me several times, trying to get things going again, but I never followed up. That was that. I regret so much that we didn't. We could have helped so many families. We could have worked with and gotten to know Dr. Lawrence. Why do people let things like money or power shove them off track?"

She opened her eyes and looked over at the old storyteller, but it was no longer him sitting there on the bench next to her. She jumped, startled.

A young soldier sat beside her, his battle fatigues dirty, his helmet in his lap. His head was down on his chest and he appeared to be crying softly.

"Sorry, ma'am. I'm still getting used to all this, I guess." He wiped his eyes with dirty hands and set the helmet down on the bench between them, where the old man's wax-paper-wrapped sandwich had been only seconds before. "I'm new to this. Sorry."

"But where did…the older gentleman…the man who was just…?"

"Oh, you mean Claude? He and Celia have been doing this for a long time, talking to folks and all, telling them the stories they need to hear about some of the people buried out here. I'm just getting started. I'm new on the job."

The young soldier sniffed and wiped at his eyes

again. The tears and dirt streaked his cheeks. He looked so young. So very young. Diana could not imagine the military was selecting such young soldiers for burial duty. Or, worse, to dig the graves of soldiers who were being buried here in this cemetery. Digging graves in battle fatigues in this heat? That did not make sense either.

But then again, nothing that had happened since she entered the gates of the cemetery made sense.

She looked away so as not to embarrass the young soldier, watching the gathering rain clouds past the far end of the rows of crosses. Then she noticed for the first time a truck and backhoe and some men who were working, digging a new grave, on the horizon at the distant side of the cemetery, several hundred yards away. Two other men appeared to be erecting a tent nearby. They were silhouetted against the darkening sky.

"Is that what you've been doing, helping dig that grave?" she asked him.

"Oh, no, ma'am. That wouldn't be right."

Maybe he was part of some kind of honor guard, then. A guide for visitors to the cemetery, maybe? She did not ask, though. His uniform was filthy, muddy.

There even appeared to be dried blood all over the front of his blouse. If he was a tour guide or part of an honor guard, he really should have avoided the bar fight or whatever catastrophe it was that left him looking so disheveled. He was probably about to be in some deep trouble with his commanding officer, showing up for duty like that.

"Did you know the soldier they are getting ready to bury, then? Is that why you are so sad?" she asked.

He slowly turned toward her. He had the most amazing blue eyes she had ever seen, and with all the dirt and sweat on his face, they seemed to glow. He smiled then, a tentative one, and then it changed into a full grin.

"Yeah. Yeah, I knew him. He was a real dope. I hate to speak ill of the dead, but he was a real dope." The young soldier laughed heartily. "Don't get me wrong. He wasn't mean or anything like that. He was just full of mischief and couldn't be serious about anything for long. He had some great folks who loved him a lot. His name was Robert Lovell. Grew up in Vina, Alabama. His grandparents made him go to church but he would sneak out and go fishing with his buddies instead, or have somebody buy him a six-pack of beer and he'd go hang out at the swimming hole instead of going to preaching. He liked hunting and fishing a whole lot better than Sunday school and prayer meeting or going to school."

"Sounds like he needed to grow up," Diana offered.

"Well, he finally grew up all right. And not a minute too soon." The young soldier eased back on the bench and cleared his throat. "You got a minute, maybe I can practice my storytelling on you, ma'am. It is a short one, not especially different from a lot of others, but I think you—of all people—will get something out of it."

Yet again, she looked back at her car, the street, the time on her PDA, worried about where she should be, what she should be taking care of. Robbie's soccer match. She never actually intended to go. And she needed to return the calls from Jeff's cell phone. What time was it in Iraq if it was 1:37 PM in Nashville, Tennessee?

It suddenly occurred to her that something might have happened to Jeff. But that thought was overcome by the realization that something very

strange was going on there in that cemetery. Time seemed to have stopped.

She shook the cell phone but the time on its impartial screen remained the same. She checked the expensive designer watch on her wrist. The times all matched. Celia talked for a good forty-five minutes. Old Claude's part of the story had taken at least a half hour. It should be almost 3 o'clock. Not more than five minutes had passed since she first sat down on that shaded bench and encountered Celia.

An odd sensation ran through her, warmer than a chill. Maybe time stood still in this peaceful place. She had lost all perspective. She was suddenly too dizzy to even consider making a run for the car, calling a taxi or somebody from the office to come get her.

The songbird was serenading them again. The breeze off the rainstorm was warm, damp, and sweet-scented. She relaxed. She wriggled her toes in the grass. The young soldier was still sitting there next to her.

"OK," she heard herself saying. "I guess I have time for just one more tall tale."

The Hero

The young soldier began his story haltingly, shyly, as if he was unsure of how the words were supposed to line up and fit together. However, as he talked, he slipped into his deep southern accent and quickly became more comfortable. He seemed to know the story well and was anxious to share it with somebody who would listen.

"Ma'am, I want to tell you about a boy who had no idea of where he was going in life or how he was going to get back home if he actually made it to his destination," he told her. "I want to tell you how one man made a big difference in the boy's life and set him on the right road before it was too late. The boy's name was Robert Lovell."

Robert was a self-described redneck and proud of it. School certainly held no interest for him. He planned on dropping out as soon as his grandparents, the people who raised him, would allow it. However, the simple fact that he would have had to

work dawn to dark on his granddad's farm propelled him out of bed each morning so he could catch the school bus.

Church was the same. Granddad told him he could stay home from Sunday school and preaching anytime he wanted to. But that was only if he painted the barn, plowed up the hayfield, and shoveled out the chicken house. If Robert did not believe the part about going to church then he did not believe the part about resting on the Sabbath, his grandfather told him. Still, even though he continued to show up, Lovell paid little attention to what he heard and failed to learn much at either school or church.

Then, with the attack on the World Trade Center in New York, Robert suddenly became aware of a world out there beyond the deer stand and the best fishing spots on the Tennessee River. A cousin went to fight in Afghanistan and came back with stories of all the good things they were doing over there on the other side of the globe. Glorified stories of adventures, too. Half because he felt a duty to defend his country and half because he liked the idea of carrying a rifle for something other than plugging squirrels, Robert went down to the recruiting office and tried to join the Army. His grades were too bad and he did not do well on the aptitude tests. Finally, when there was an opening, he re-tested and joined the nearest National Guard unit. Not long after he returned home from his basic training, Robert's group was called up. Soon they knew that they were headed for the war in Iraq.

He saw worry in his grandmother's eyes. His granddad took him aside and, for the first time in his life, told him—out loud—how much he loved him. His granddad slipped a Charlie Daniels Band CD into his suitcase. He had marked one particular song, "The Last Fallen Hero," and a note attached with a rubber band that said, "Don't forget this is why you are going over yonder." The song, sung in the artist's usual gruff voice, was about avenging the deaths of those innocent people lost on September 11, as well as the brave soldiers who had died already, trying to exact some justice for all those wasted lives—the perfect theme song for Robert's quest.

Robert Lovell was not a spectacular soldier at all. Not even a very good one. He tried his best because he did not want to let his buddies down or put them into danger, but he simply had a difficult time with

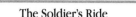
the discipline, the spit-and-polish part of the military. He sometimes had troulble understanding orders or seeing the need for doing some of the things he was told to do, especially early in boot camp when the orders simply made no sense to him. Instead of jumping when told to jump, he pondered the command until the superior who gave it screamed at him and ordered him to do push-ups—him and his entire squad, making him unpopular with the other men.

His commander in Iraq simply called him a "free spirit."

"Lovell, why you back there picking daisies?" he called. "Double-time on up here with the rest of us before the war is over!"

When they were on patrol, Robert had a tendency to linger behind the others, simply to watch kids play games in a dusty field or observe a pack of rats stage an assault on a garbage heap. Or he would wander outside the perimeter they had set up just to pick up a wild alley cat, then attempt to pet and feed it. He told jokes but forgot the punch lines. He tried to remember Bible verses but got them all scrambled. He was gullible and often the victim of pranks from

the other members of his platoon. It was easy to put one over on "Free Spirit." Besides, he rarely got mad or tried to retaliate, no matter how cruel the joke.

His commander took a special interest in him, though, and worked with him to help him be a better soldier. He told Robert he was concentrating on him because he did not want him to wander off into a minefield or go lollygagging right into the middle of an ambush someday. Whatever his reason, his leader saw something in the kid and helped Robert be a better person, too. When the young man got to thinking about home and seemed on the verge of tears, or was clearly afraid, his captain talked with him, read to him from the Bible, prayed with him. Robert assumed his leader did not want the others to see him cry.

But it worked. He was getting better at soldiering. He did not miss his grandparents or the woods and streams back home as much as he once did. Somehow, the words and explanations about the things he and his commander read in the Bible together made him feel less afraid, too. He found comfort in prayer, though he still did not do it aloud or so the other guys could hear him.

He figured God could hear them and that was what mattered. He was still too shy, too uncomfortable, to talk with anyone else about his newly found religion.

Private Robert Lovell was part of a squad of six sent out one night to investigate a house in a neighborhood north of Baghdad. The house was supposed to be a hideout for several known insurgents, a place where roadside bombs were being built to kill and maim American troops. As the squad neared the target hut, Robert lingered for only a moment to study a small vegetable garden he noticed. The garden struggled to take root in the dusty front yard of the hut next door to the one they were supposed to check on.

Among other things, Robert Lovell sorely missed his grandmother's fried okra, sliced tomatoes, and fresh peas, all of it just picked from her garden and served with her hot, buttery cornbread. Nothing in this garden resembled tomatoes or okra, so he lost interest.

A woman and her two children walked by then. One of the children held a small, wriggling puppy in his arms. Robert held up his hands to show he

meant no harm and stepped over to pet the dog. The boy smiled when his pup wagged his tail and licked the soldier's hand while it squirmed, trying to get away. Robert grinned, ruffled the boy's hair, and waved 'bye to them. Then the boy and the rest of his family walked on.

At that point, Robert realized the others in his squad were well ahead of him, about to reach the target house. He turned and started running to catch up with the squad.

Suddenly, he saw something skittering along the ground in front of the house, rolling toward where his squad was about to break up to begin encircling the suspect structure. Lovell knew at once what it was—a grenade—and none of the others had seen it. Someone inside the place must have spotted their approach, probably forewarned by somebody in the neighborhood, and tossed the grenade out a window toward Robert's buddies.

But Robert saw more. There were others there, too, who were in danger. The woman and her two children were by then approaching the American soldiers. The boy's puppy had jumped from his arms and was yapping at the Americans in their strange combat outfits. The kid was running, calling for the dog, trying to retrieve it. The soldiers were laughing, trying to hem up the animal, too.

"Free Spirit" did not hesitate. He screamed loud enough to send his buddies into a sudden dive for cover. They could still be hurt. The grenades typically threw ugly, sharp fragments twirling and slashing a good thirty feet when they exploded. But the woman and children were stunned by the crazy, whooping soldier bearing down on them and the sudden dive for cover by the other Americans.

The woman, likely mother of the two children, dropped down to her knees, right where she stood, encircling the children and the yelping puppy in her arms, trying to shield them from whatever was happening.

The live grenade was only a few feet away from them.

Without hesitation, Lovell threw himself down in the dusty street between the civilians and the spot where the grenade had now rolled to a stop. Protecting the woman and kids with his body, he tried to pick up the deadly thing. His intention was to toss it back toward the hut, away from them all.

He was too late. It blew up, slinging metal, before he could even get enough of a grip on it to throw it away.

Screaming in terror but unhurt, the woman and her children ran. One squad member caught a jagged fragment from the grenade in his thigh and went down hard. The others were okay. The quick, brave action taken by one member of their squad saved their lives.

Robert "Free Spirit" Lovell, though, was dead.

The Soldier

"I suppose you guessed that the hole they're digging over yonder is for Private Robert Lovell," the young soldier said quietly, nodding toward the activity at the far side of the field. "That soldier's ride will end on a caisson pulled by a team of horses at four o'clock this afternoon. Private Lovell might not have been the best soldier, like Christopher Wren Lawrence or Josiah Malone or some of the others that have crosses here. Or Celia Crawford or Claude Sadler. But he laid down his life for his country, for his buddies, and for that innocent woman and her children, who just happened to be in a bad place that night. For all those people in that skyscraper that everyday morning. For the sailors, still asleep in their bunks on the USS *Arizona* in Pearl Harbor when that Japanese bomb went right through the deck and blew up in the magazine. That's what soldiers do, ma'am."

Diana Meade swallowed the lump in her throat.

She had too many questions to ask. She did not know where to start.

"Wait. You mentioned Celia and Claude, the old folks who were here before. They were soldiers, too?"

"Yes ma'am. Claude was on submarines. He helped pull over three dozen American fliers out of the Pacific Ocean when their bombers went down off the coast of Japan. They were under constant threat from airplanes and patrol boats, but he was up there on that slippery deck, pulling those fly-boys out of the water. Claude was on the submarine that sank the *Shinano*, the biggest ship ever sunk by a submarine. That was supposed to be an unsinkable aircraft carrier, but he and his shipmates sank her with six torpedoes. Sometimes God does take sides. He only served two years but he was a soldier. A sailor to be exact.

"And Celia? She was a Navy nurse. She was in Pearl Harbor the day the Japanese attacked, but she spent most of the war on some little island in the middle of the ocean. She helped a lot of soldiers get better and she watched hundreds of them die, and she did a lot of that with the enemy still shelling them from the mountains. Then, just to make sure she did her duty, she was at a hospital in Korea for a year, too. You won't see either of their names in the history books. Neither of them talked much about it, not even when they first got out here to this place. It was not long, though, before they started bringing folks like you up to date, telling you what you needed to know so you might understand things better."

"Folks like me? Understand things?"

"I don't mean to offend you, ma'am, but folks don't understand sometimes why men…and women, too…must go to war. Why they sacrifice for their country and the things they believe in. Ma'am, very few fighting men or women go to war gladly. They go because they must. Your husband, Captain Meade, he could have left the Guard a long time ago. I figure he don't need the money. He could have gone over to the AG side, what with his law degree and all and he never would have had to leave the States. He could have been promoted, too. I heard he turned down two promotions because he wanted to stay with his men if and when they were deployed to a war zone. He did it because he knew somebody had to."

The young soldier paused for breath. He was sitting upright now, his back straight, his jaw out to emphasize the import of his words.

"Your husband could have kept his religion to himself, too, but he shared it with all of us because he knew it was important that we know the truth. Your husband was the best commander a soldier like me could ever have. It was not his fault what happened. I was a few steps behind my squad that night for a purpose. A purpose that only God knew at the time."

Diana looked hard at him. He was looking back at her with those bluer-than-blue eyes, and he had a slight smile on his dirt-and-tear-smeared face.

Then she saw the name across his uniform pocket.

"Lovell."

The sudden roar in her ears blocked out the distant rumble of thunder. Her mouth fell open. The breath left her body. She felt disoriented, dizzy.

But before she could get enough air back into her lungs to ask the question that was on her lips, she did hear something. Something so familiar that grabbed her heart and caused it to miss a beat.

It was the shout of a child.

Her child. Robbie.

"Mom! Mom!"

The Funeral

He was running toward her from the entrance gate, a soccer ball under his arm, his long, blonde hair blowing in the breeze. She stood and stepped forward to meet him.

"Robbie? How did you...?"

"We won, Mom. We won our game. I scored a goal!"

"That's great, honey, but how did you get up here?"

Then she saw him. Jeff. Her husband. He was walking their way slowly, limping just a bit. He was in his dress uniform. Similar to the ROTC uniform he was wearing the first time she met him and fell instantly in love with him.

"I tried to call you," he said, nodding toward the purse on her arm where her cell phone hid.

Without even thinking about it, she hugged him, holding him close for a moment. She had missed him. If she had given herself the chance, if she had allowed herself enough time for emotion, she would have missed him to the point of pain.

"I'm sorry. But how did you know where I was?"

"I called your office. They told me you broke down here. But I was coming this way anyway." Jeff nodded again, this time toward where the gravediggers were just finishing up their sad job. People were already gathering near the tent. The storm seemed to have blown itself out, but there was still a refreshing breeze and the clouds dented the sun's rays. "We're burying one of my boys today."

"I know. Private Lovell." Diana glanced back to the shaded bench but she knew already that nobody would be there. She smiled. "I guess I read it in the paper. I didn't know you would be here, though."

"I e-mailed you on the personal account. Left you messages, too, but I didn't know for sure that I would be able to travel until..."

She stood away from him and looked him up and down.

"What happened? Are you okay?"

"Aw, I'm fine. I took some shrapnel in the thigh and then I got a nasty infection. They wanted to keep me in Germany but I had to be here," he said.

"The kid we're burying today..."

"Saved your life," she said quietly.

"What?"

"The kid you're burying today saved your life," Diana said, her eyes filled with tears. "He fell on that grenade."

Now Jeff's mouth dropped open.

"That part was never in the paper. Not the details. How did you know that?"

Diana eyes filled with tears.

"Let's just say an angel told me. He told me that and a lot more, too." She pulled him close again and kissed him on the cheek. Robbie was kicking the soccer ball around a green patch between the graves but he stopped and stared at them. He could not remember the last time he saw his parents embracing. "Do you think it would be okay if I went to the funeral with you?"

"I'm sure it would, but don't you have to get back to the office?"

A tow truck sat in front of her lifeless automobile, the driver looking around for its owner with a puzzled look on his face.

"No. No, I don't. I need to go to this funeral, Jeff.

I have to go."

Jeff hobbled over to tell the tow truck driver where he could deliver Diana's car then drove his own vehicle back to pick up her and their son. She found her heels beneath the bench but there were no signs anybody else had been there in the shade with her.

Then she saw the small stone, almost lost in the grass. It was her courage stone. The one she thought she had lost. It must have fallen out of the little compartment in her purse where she kept her cell phone.

She sat on the bench again to wait for her husband and watched Robbie recreating his winning soccer goal amid the graves of the heroes. A strange feeling washed over her. A pleasant feeling. A feeling of contentment she had not felt in years. She held the smooth stone in her fingers and, before she knew it, she was doing something that felt mighty close to saying a prayer. It had been so long she could not be sure.

Jeff rolled to a stop. She left the bench, walked to the car, and she slid in next to him. Robbie came running and jumped into the back seat. Slowly, a family reunited for this tragic event, they rode along the narrow paved roadway between the rows and rows of crosses. Jeff found a parking place among the others who were arriving for the service.

Diana saw an old couple just getting out of an ancient pickup truck, leaning on each other as if they could not walk alone. She wore a black dress and veil, he an ill-fitting black suit. She knew at once these people must be Private Lovell's grandparents, the ones who raised him and sent him off to war. She was about to step over and offer to help them negotiate the slight rise to where the earth was opened up, but she knew she could never tell them about meeting their grandson.

The old couple stopped, held hands, bowed their heads a quick moment, and then stood taller, straighter, as if that pause strengthened them mightily. Still holding hands, they walked up the hill with vigor and found their seats on the front row of chairs aligned beneath the tent.

Diana looked up at Jeff and smiled. He had seen the same thing and smiled at her. She dropped her head, closed her eyes and said a quick prayer of thanks to God for sending Jeff back to her. There was no doubt about it this time. She was actually praying. It felt natural, though it was the first time in decades.

When she looked up at her ex-husband, he was grinning widely.

"Did you just say a prayer?" he asked her.

"Yes. Yes, I did. I thanked God for your being here. For Private Lovell and what he did. For what all these men and women buried in this place did." She took his hand in hers. "Jeff, I need to talk with you when you have a chance. I have so much to tell you. You won't believe some of it, but you have to listen, Jeff. I have so many things I want to make right."

He looked at her, his eyes squinting, obviously wondering about her, about what happened.

Before she could say more or he could ask her any of the questions he wanted to, there was a sound from down the hill, near the gate. Bagpipes playing "Amazing Grace." The clip-clop of horses' hoofs on pavement, the horses drawing a caisson. The taps on the boots of the honor guard marching close behind and the sing-song sound of the squad leader calling cadence.

Diana turned, one of her hands in Jeff's, her

son's hand in the other, and walked up the hill toward the tent. Dozens of people stood there. Some wore uniforms and nodded to Jeff. Several saluted. Others were dressed casually, like the farmers and millworkers they were.

Both rows of chairs next to the grave were filled with relatives of the young soldier, including the older couple. Their hands were still intertwined and despite the nature of the occasion, they had a look of infinite peace on their faces as they watched the casket of their grandson slowly approach up the winding roadway behind the horses. The worn Bible rested in the old man's lap, open to what must have been a verse that had special meaning to them.

The Meades found a spot nearby, close enough to hear the minister's words and at a position where they could watch the riflemen and their salute.

"Your leg? You need to find a bench?" she suddenly thought to ask Jeff.

"No. It's fine. I owe it to that boy to stand and that's what I am going to do."

Then Diana glanced back toward the gravesite and her legs suddenly went limp. There, just beyond the opening in the black earth, just past the few people who stood there on the other side of the tent, three figures stood away from the others.

Celia, Claude, and Robert Lovell, standing side-by-side, as if they had just walked up the hill with the rest of the mourners, watching the slowly approaching caisson, waiting for the service to start.

Claude in his overalls, leaning on the leaf rake.

Celia in her sweater and long dress.

Robert Lovell still in his dirty, bloodstained fatigues.

They all turned as one and looked approvingly at Diana and her reunited family. They waved and smiled at her in a way that implied that they were all four sharing a glorious secret.

She looked up at Jeff to see if he had seen the trio. He was watching the coffin as the honor guard lifted it from the short, horse-drawn wagon and marched with the true hero it held toward his body's final resting place.

When she looked back to where the angels had been, they were gone.

A hundred feet away, beneath the shade of another tall elm, a lone trumpeter raised his instrument to his lips and began playing "Taps."

A Miracle in Me

Fear can't keep me in this valley.
The weight of doubt won't hold me down.
Someone's out there watching over me.
I'll rest in the peace I've found.

    I believe in miracles.
    I have seen what the power of love can do.
    Prayers keep me hanging on
    And hope, hope will see me through.
    I walk in faith and trust in things
    I can't even see
    'Cause I believe there's a miracle in me.

Nothing in this world can break me,
But I've come close a time or two.
I've felt the storms before the healing.
Those storms, they led me straight to you.

Now I believe in miracles.
I have seen what the power of love can do.
Prayers keep me hanging on
And hope, hope will see me through.
I walk in faith and trust in things
I can't even see
'Cause I believe there's a miracle in me

©2008 Waldron, Hargrove, Harris, Rickles. Used by permission.
Mark Waldron [Acoustic Scribbles Music/BMI]
(www.acousticscribbles.com)
Jack Hargrove [Vick's Picks Publishing/BMI]
Ashley Harris [Revitalize Publishing/BMI] (www.ashleyharris.com)
Vicki Rickles [Vick's Picks Publishing/BMI]

The Cookin' Colonel's Recipes

Seafood Gumbo

¼ cup olive oil
¼ cup all-purpose flour
1 large onion, chopped
1 medium green bell pepper, chopped
¼ cup chopped garlic, finely minced
¾ cup seafood stock (see below)
2 bay leaves
1 teaspoon Worcestershire sauce
Juice of ½ lemon
1 teaspoon dried thyme leaves
1 teaspoon dried sweet basil leaves
1 teaspoon dried oregano leaves
1 teaspoon freshly ground black pepper
½ teaspoon cayenne pepper
Salt to taste
1 pound lump crabmeat, (picked through for any
        remaining pieces of shell)
2 pounds raw shrimp, peeled and deveined
1 pint oysters
1 pound redfish or red snapper fillets,
        cut in bite-size nuggets
1 pound bay scallops
3 cups hot cooked rice
1 jar filé powder (optional)
½ cup fresh chopped green onions for garnish
½ cup fresh chopped parsley for garnish

In a large, heavy cast-iron skillet heat the olive oil over medium heat and add the flour, stirring constantly to make a dark brown roux. Add the onion, bell pepper, celery, and garlic, cooking until the vegetables are nice and soft, about 5 minutes.

Meanwhile, in a large saucepan, bring the stock to a boil. Slowly whisk the roux into boiling stock until all the following have been added. Add the bay leaves, Worcestershire sauce, and lemon juice along with the herbs and spices. Reduce the heat and simmer 2 hours.

Add the crabmeat, shrimp, oysters, fish, and scallops. Cook over medium heat for 5 minutes. Taste for seasoning; adjust if necessary.

To serve, place a small amount of rice in each bowl and spoon out some of the gumbo on top of it. Sprinkle with a little bit of the filè powder and stir to make the gumbo thick. Garnish with the fresh chopped green onions and parsley.

Serves 8, but multiply the ingredients by three or four or more to make enough to serve those who may not have enough to eat. Before enjoying, be sure to say grace with a humble heart, thanking God for allowing you the wonderful meal you are about to enjoy and for blessing you in so many ways.

"And if you spend yourselves in behalf of the hungry and satisfy the needs of the oppressed, then your light will rise in the darkness, and your night will become like the noonday." Isaiah 58:10

Cajun Cornbread

1 cup sifted enriched flour
1 cup yellow cornmeal
2 eggs beaten
1 cup whole milk
4 tsp baking powder
¾ tsp salt
¼ cup shortening
¼ cup cane sugar

Sift together the flour, cane sugar, baking powder, salt, and cornmeal. blending very well. Next, add in the eggs, whole milk, and the shortening and beat together until all is just nicely smooth. (An electric mixer works very well for this.) Now, pour the mixture into a greased baking pan and bake in the oven at 425 degrees for about 20 to 25 minutes.

Double or triple the recipe and bake two or three pones of cornbread at the same time so you can give some to those who either do not have enough or who are unable to cook for themselves. God will bless you many times over.

"Put the bread of the Presence on this table to be before me at all times." Exodus 25:30

Cajun Creole Seafood Dip

1 Cup sour cream
1 Cup mayonnaise
8 Ounces fresh lump crabmeat
¼ Pound fresh cooked shrimp, chopped up
¼ Cup green onions, chopped
¼ Cup chopped celery
1 Tbsp lemon juice
¼ Cup chopped fresh parsley
¼ Cup chopped fresh thyme
1 tsp chopped fresh garlic

Seasoning Mix
2 Tbsp of your favorite Cajun/Creole seasoning blend or:

½ tsp ground thyme
½ tsp ground sweet basil
¼ tsp salt
½ tsp garlic powder
½ tsp onion powder
¼ tsp black pepper
¼ tsp white pepper
¼ tsp cayenne pepper
1 tsp sweet paprika

Combine all ingredients in a mixing bowl and blend very well. The longer that the dip sets the more flavorful it will become. This recipe can be made a day before and kept in the refrigerator in a sealed container overnight to make it more flavorful still. As the dip warms up to room temperature, it will taste even better. Serve in a nice bowl with some crackers or sliced carrots or celery.

Do not forget to thank God for providing such a wonderful taste treat, and for blessing you with the ability to create delicious food for you, your friends, guests, and family.

"For I was hungry and you gave me something to eat, I was thirsty and you gave me something to drink, I was a stranger and you invited me in." Matthew 25:35

About the Authors

Edie Hand is one of those remarkable people who brightens up a room as soon as she walks in. Her philosophy for living life with gusto can be seen in everything she does from her work as an acclaimed celebrity chef, author, philanthropist, speaker and business woman.

Edie learned about the simple joys of family, life and helping others from her modest childhood growing up in the rural south. She is a cousin to the late Elvis Presley and also the cousin of 2007 Nashville Star winner, Angela Hacker. She has authored, co-authored and assisted in the development of over twenty books. Her books range from inspirational cookbooks to novellas.

Edie has starred in national commercials and daytime television soaps. She has hosted numerous national radio and television shows and been the CEO of Hand 'N Hand Advertising, Inc. since 1976.

Edie is actively involved with American Women of Radio and Television, National Speakers Association, National Association of Women Business Owners and has worked to benefit the Children's Hospital of Alabama, Children's Miracle Network, St. Jude Children's Research Hospital, Camp Smile-A-Mile and Country Music Hall of Fame Foundation. She is a graduate of the University of North Alabama.

Edie lives near Birmingham, Alabama with her husband Mark Aldridge, an educator. Her only son, Linc Hand, a working actor, lives in Los Angeles, California.

For more information, go to these websites:
www.ediehand.com
www.ediehandfoundation.org

Jeffery Addison is one of the pen names of award-winning broadcast journalist, radio personality, and best selling author Don Keith. Don has seventeen books in print, including novels and non-fiction works. His latest book, *The Ice Diaries*, has been submitted for consideration for the Pulitzer Prize. His military thriller, *Firing Point*, has been optioned as a major motion picture by Relativity Films and is now in pre-production. In addition to his writing, he is a marketing executive and runs a full-service advertising and public relations agency. He lives with his wife, Charlene, in Indian Springs Village, Alabama.

Visit his web sites for more information:
www.jefferyaddisonbooks.com
www.donkeith.com